Camp Club Girls

Elizabeth's
Amarillo Adventure

To Charis, Mom, and Carolyn.
Thanks for teaching the meaning of true friendship.
I love all of you!

Edited by Jeanette Littleton.

ISBN 978-1-60260-290-8

Cover design: Thinkpen Design

Published by Barbour Publishing, Inc., P.O. Box 719, Uhrichsville, Ohio 44683, www.barbourbooks.com

Our mission is to publish and distribute inspirational products offering exceptional value and biblical encouragement to the masses.

ecpa Member of the Evangelical Christian Publishers Association

Printed in the United States of America.
Dickinson Press; Grand Rapids, MI; May 2010; D10002361

Camp Club Girls

Elizabeth's Amarillo Adventure

Renae Brumbaugh

BARBOUR
PUBLISHING

The Mystery Marbles

"Elizabeth! Come quick! My grandmother has lost her marbles!"

Elizabeth held the phone out from her ear, trying to understand what her friend was saying. "Megan, what are you talking about? I thought your grandmother was dead!"

"She is! Listen, you've got to get down here right now." Megan hung up the phone, leaving Elizabeth baffled.

Elizabeth replaced the phone on its base and dashed out the door. As an afterthought, she stepped back inside and grabbed a letter off the entryway table. Cramming it in her back pocket, she called out, "Mom, I'm going to see Megan—I'll be back in a little while!" She slipped her helmet on, jumped on her bike, and headed down the driveway.

"Wait!" her mother cried, and Elizabeth slammed on her brakes. The screen door squeaked as Mrs. Anderson stepped onto the porch, drying a coffee mug with a white dish towel. "I thought Megan was at work."

"She is, but she gets her break at 2:30. That was her

on the phone, and she wants me to come," Elizabeth said, adjusting her helmet.

Mrs. Anderson continued drying the mug, and looked at her daughter a moment. "Okay, but be careful crossing streets, and come straight back here after Megan's break is over."

"Yes, ma'am," Elizabeth called as she lunged her bike forward. She practically flew the four blocks to the restaurant. If it hadn't been for the pesky stops she had to make at the intersections, she could have made it in half the time. But safety first.

Within minutes, she parked her bicycle next to her friend's scooter, near the back entrance. Going to the front of the restaurant, she pushed open the heavy door. The restaurant seemed black, compared to the bright Texas sunlight. It took her a moment to adjust her vision, and she looked around.

Jean Louise, the head waitress, greeted her with a wink. "You're just in time, girly. Megan just sat down at her usual table," she drawled.

"Thanks," Elizabeth told her. She sidled through the mixture of cowboys and tourists who were the customers at the Big Texan Steak Ranch.

"What took you so long?" Megan asked as she stood to greet her friend.

Elizabeth slid into the booth and said, "I got here as fast as I could. What's up with your grandmother?"

"I have no idea. Jean Louise is telling me some crazy story about my grandmother and some marbles and us being rich or something. That's all I know. And since you're the mystery girl, I called you."

Elizabeth didn't know what to say. Sure, she had helped solve mysteries with the Camp Club Girls, but she was surprised Megan would even remember that.

Megan leaned her chin on her hands then. "I'm exhausted. We've been busier than usual today. I've washed more dishes today than I have in my entire life! I'm just too tired to try to solve a mystery."

Elizabeth grinned. "Yeah, but just think of all that cash you'll have when you collect your first paycheck!"

Megan put her head on the table and moaned. "All I can think about right now is my tired back." After a few seconds, she sat up and added, "But it will be nice to be able to buy my saxophone. I know Mom can't afford it, and I don't want to ask her. But I really want to be in the band."

Jean Louise set a tall glass of iced tea in front of Megan. "What'll ya have?" she asked Elizabeth.

"Oh, nothing. I just—"

"Nonsense. It's on the house. Just tell me what you want," the tall redheaded waitress said around her gum.

Elizabeth paused, realizing the woman wouldn't take no for an answer. "I'll have a root beer," she said politely.

Jean Louise winked and said, "One root beer, coming up!"

Megan sat up and smiled at her friend. "I'm sorry. I haven't even asked about your day."

Megan and Elizabeth had grown up more like sisters than next-door neighbors. Though Megan was a year and a half older, she and Elizabeth had played together, walked to school together, and gone to church together for as long as they could remember.

Elizabeth pulled the letter from her back pocket and slid it across the table. "It's from my friend McKenzie. I told you about her—from camp? She's the one from Montana, the one who has horses. She's wanted to visit Texas, and she's finally going to. Her family is coming here to Amarillo for their vacation! She's coming to visit!"

Megan opened the envelope and pulled out the pages. She skimmed the contents of the letter, and then handed it back to Elizabeth. "That's great, Beth, really. I'm excited for you."

Both girls sat silently for a moment.

"And I promise to act excited, as soon as I have slept about forty hours," Megan continued with a yawn.

Just then, Jean Louise appeared with the root beer and two oversize pieces of apple pie, topped with enormous scoops of ice cream. "Here ya' go," she said.

Both girls perked up at the sight of the pie. "Wow! Thanks, Jean Louise!" they told her.

"Awww, hush up now. No need to thank me. You've

earned that and more. You just eat and enjoy your break," she told Megan. She turned to go, then changed her mind. "So, what are you going to do about that special tip?"

Megan, whose mouth was poised for her first juicy bite of pie, stopped. "Well, actually, that's why I called Elizabeth. She's good at solving these kinds of things."

The waitress turned to Elizabeth. "So, you'll help her solve this mystery, huh?"

"I'm not sure," said Elizabeth. "First, I need to know more about those marbles."

"Shhhhh!" Jean Louise looked around her, as if not wanting anyone to overhear. "Honey, we need to talk. But not here. These walls have ears. Why don't you two head over to my place after work today?"

Megan nodded, and the waitress moved to take an order from the next table. "So, can you come?" the girl asked.

Elizabeth thought a moment. "I'll have to ask my mom. I'm supposed to stay with James while Mom and Dad go to a meeting at church, but maybe he can go with them."

"Okay. Meet me at the back door if you can," Megan told her. The girls finished their pie and drinks without much further conversation. Elizabeth was still thinking about this new mystery, and Megan was just too tired to talk.

•—•—•

Mrs. Anderson stood in her kitchen, looking between Elizabeth and six-year-old James, who were both talking.

"Megan wants me to go with her to Jean Louise's house at six," Elizabeth told her mother.

"Elizabeth promised she would watch me tonight, Mom! I want her to stay with me," James interrupted his sister.

"I know I said I'd watch him, but I think this is really important to Megan," Elizabeth continued. "Something about a special tip and her grandmother."

"But I wanted Beth to help me finish my Lego airplane. It's more fun when she helps me," James urged. "Make her stay with me. . .please!"

Elizabeth held in an exasperated sigh. She loved James. She just didn't like being his full-time playmate. She needed her space, and he didn't want to give it to her.

Mrs. Anderson looked at Elizabeth, then at James. "I don't think Elizabeth promised you anything, James. I asked her to stay with you tonight, and she agreed. But Josh's mom called earlier and is bringing Josh with her tonight, so you'll have a playmate."

James's face brightened as he said, "Cool! I'll go pack my toys so we can play!"

"You may take two toys, and that's it!" Mrs. Anderson called after him. Then she looked at her daughter.

Elizabeth slowly released her breath. She was off the hook with James, but she still didn't have permission to go with Megan.

"Is this Jean Louise Wilson, the waitress at the Big

Texan?" her mother asked.

"Yes, ma'am. She's the tall lady with red hair. She gave us free pie today."

"I know her. She's nice," her mother said. She stood, clearly trying to make up her mind. "Okay, but you need to leave her house by seven thirty. I want you home before dark. And you girls stay together. If we're not home by the time you get back, go to Megan's house with her. We should be back around eight."

Elizabeth gave her mother a tight hug. "Oh, thank you, thank you, thank you! You're the best mom in the world!" She kissed her mother's cheek and ran to her room.

At 5:58 p.m., Elizabeth sat on the back stoop of the Big Texan Steak Ranch waiting for her friend. At 6:01 p.m., the back door opened, Megan stepped outside and collapsed next to her friend.

"I'm not sure what I've gotten myself into," Megan told her. "Washing dishes here is a lot harder than washing dishes at home. They just keep coming and coming, and I can never get caught up!"

"I'll bet you'll get faster, the more you do it," Elizabeth encouraged her. "Besides, just think of the free pie!"

"Speaking of free pie, the cook sent these home with me," Megan answered, nodding toward two pie-sized boxes. "We'll never eat all of this, so one of them is going to your house."

"I won't argue," Elizabeth told her. "Should we drop them off before we go to Jean Louise's?"

"That's a good idea," Megan answered, and Elizabeth took the boxes from her.

"I walked, so I'll carry them. Then we can ride our bikes from home."

Soon the girls were bicycling through town, toward a section of small but well-kept hundred-year-old homes. They found the address the waitress had given them and rang the doorbell.

Jean Louise answered the door wearing cutoff jeans and a trendy T-shirt. It was an outfit that Elizabeth expected to see on a much younger person, but it looked good on the red-haired lady. The woman smacked her gum and said, "Come on in, y'all. I just made some fresh, sweet tea. And if you're hungry, I have some leftover fried chicken. You'll have to eat it cold, but that's how I like it."

The girls would have preferred to skip the tea and jump straight to the mystery, but they didn't want to be rude.

"I'll have some tea, thanks," said Megan. Elizabeth nodded that she'd have the same.

The two girls sat in the tidy, old-fashioned living room. A collection of salt and pepper shakers lined the mantel, and a pink porcelain teapot shaped like a pig rested on a tray on the coffee table. They could hear Jean Louise singing with a popular country and western song that was playing on an antique radio in the corner.

The older woman handed them the tea and placed a couple of pig-shaped coasters on the coffee table. She turned the radio down and sat across from them in a green overstuffed chair. "Megan, were you serious when you said you didn't know anything about a special tip?" she asked.

Megan set her tea down and answered, "Jean Louise, I still don't know what you're talking about. My grandmother died when my mother was a little girl."

The woman looked at her, as if deciding what she should say. "I don't mean to be nosy, honey, but why are you working as a dishwasher? Is money tight for you all?"

Megan blushed, but held her head high. "We do okay. We're not rich, but we always have what we need."

Jean Louise shifted in her chair. "Well, darlin', with that tip your grandmother got, you should have everything you need, everything you want, and then some."

Elizabeth sipped her tea and remained quiet.

"Jean Louise, you're not making any sense," Megan said to the woman.

The woman looked out the window, then back at Megan. "You're really not kidding, are you? You don't know anything about the marbles."

"Jean Louise, please tell me what in the world you're talking about," Megan responded.

"Oh, honey. Some rich fella' was head over heels in love

with Emily Marie—your grandma. I remember it like it was yesterday. I was just a young teenager myself, and the whole thing was so romantic. Your grandma and my mama were best friends, and I used to hang out at the restaurant after school, till my mama got off work. This fella came in once a week or so, and he'd always sit at the same table in your grandma's section. Then he started coming several times a week. Before long, he was visiting the restaurant every day, ordering nothing more than coffee or tea. But he always left her a twenty-dollar tip. He was smitten.

"Then one day, he gave her this bag of marbles. They were the prettiest things you ever saw! There was a red one and a blue one and a green one, just about every color of the rainbow. There must have been a dozen of them in that bag. But the prettiest one was crystal clear."

She paused and looked out the window, as if remembering.

Megan interrupted her silence and said, "So the special tip was a bag of marbles?"

Jean Louise slowly brought her gaze to Megan. "Honey, those weren't just any old marbles. But hold your horses. Let me finish the story."

The two girls leaned forward, their eyes glued on the sassy waitress.

"So, the fella gives Emily Marie this bag of marbles, and tells her to keep them in a safe place. He tells her he wants to take care of her, and he knows these marbles will give her and her children a comfortable future.

"Well, at first she didn't know what to say. After all, you can buy a bag of marbles at any old five and dime store. But she didn't want to offend him, so she just said, 'Thank you.'

"Then, she started to pour them out on the table, but he stopped her. He pulled her toward him and whispered something in her ear. I remember it plain as day. I was sitting at the table across from them. I was eavesdropping, even though I knew I wasn't supposed to. Your grandma was such a pretty lady, and I used to watch her all the time."

She shifted, and the sofa squeaked. Elizabeth had a pretty good guess what Megan was thinking. They both wanted the woman to get on with the story.

The squeaking seemed to draw Jean Louise back to the present. She laughed. "Oh, listen to me, chasin' rabbits. Anyway, when that man whispered in your grandma's ear, she turned white! She looked at the bag in her hands. Her hands started shaking and she tried to give it back to him, but he wouldn't take it. He kept saying, 'They're yours. I've already put them in your name. The paperwork is all there.' Then, she sat down in the booth with the man. That was against the rules, but she did it anyway. Just sat right down and started crying and telling him thank you over and over again.

"He kept telling her, 'Don't cry. I want to take care of you!' I thought he was going to ask her to marry him, right then and there. But a whole bunch of cowboys came in, and your grandma had to get back to work."

She looked at the girls as if she had finished her story.

Elizabeth and Megan looked at each other, then back at Jean Louise. In unison, they nearly yelled, "What was so special about the marbles?"

Jean Louise looked surprised. "Oh, I forgot that part, didn't I? Silly me. I'll tell you that right now. But first, would you like some more tea?"

Camp Club Girls on the Case

The girls responded in unison, "No, thank you!"

But Jean Louise didn't take the hint. She leaned forward, picked up her own glass, and said, "I'll just get myself some, then. I'll be right back." She went into the kitchen, while Megan and Elizabeth sat on the couch. They shared confused looks, but neither girl spoke a word. An old Oak Ridge Boys song played softly on the radio.

After a moment, Jean Louise sauntered back into the living room. "Sorry to keep you waiting. I know you're anxious to hear about those marbles. But to be perfectly honest, I'm having second thoughts about telling you all this. Maybe your mama is the one I should talk to, Megan."

Megan told her, "My mama and I tell each other everything anyway. But she's working overtime this week, so you probably won't be able to get in touch with her for a few days."

"Your mama was just a little girl when all this happened," said Jean Louise. She sipped her tea, as if considering her next words. Finally she said, "Okay, I'll tell you. But don't go spreading this around. Tell your mama, of course, but don't talk about it to all your little friends." She glanced at Elizabeth.

"I won't tell a soul, unless Megan wants me to," Elizabeth responded.

Megan said, "Our lips are sealed."

Finally, the woman said, "The marbles were formed out of priceless gemstones. The red one was a ruby, the blue one a sapphire, and the clear one. . .a diamond!"

The two girls looked at each other wide-eyed, and then stood to their feet and squealed. "We're rich! We're rich!" Megan sang as she hopped up and down.

The older woman let the girls have a moment before she interrupted them. "Not so fast, Megan. If you're so rich, why is your mama working so much overtime? Why are you working as a dishwasher so you can buy a band instrument?"

Surprised, Megan looked at the waitress. "How did you know that?" she asked.

"I already told you I'm an eavesdropper!" Jean Louise said with a laugh. Then she grew serious. "There's one more thing you need to know. The reason I thought about those marbles after all these years, is because a man came into the restaurant the other day asking questions."

"What kinds of questions?" asked Elizabeth, shifting into her detective mode.

"He asked to see the restaurant manager. He wanted to know if anybody knew anything about some marbles that were given to a waitress there, years ago. Of course the manager didn't know anything. We've had so many managers since that time. And your grandma never told anyone except my mama about them."

"I wonder who would be looking for them, after all this time?" asked Megan.

Jean Louise snorted. "Honey, plenty o' folks will be looking for them if they know they're missing!"

Soon the girls thanked their hostess and started home. "What should we do?" asked Megan.

"I don't know. This is your mystery, not mine. I promised Jean Louise I'd stay out of it, remember?"

"No, you didn't. You promised not to tell anybody about it. That doesn't mean you can't help me solve the mystery," her friend said.

"I don't know, Megan. This one seems over my head. I wouldn't know where to begin," Elizabeth told her.

"Come on, Beth, you've got to help me. You're the one with all the sleuthing experience," Megan urged.

Elizabeth remained quiet, as if thinking it over. "Well. . . okay! I'll do it! But first thing, we need to let your mom know what's going on."

"Okay. I'll tell her as soon as—oh, wait! She works late tonight, and I have to be at work early tomorrow. I won't even see her until tomorrow night. But I'll tell her as soon as I can, I promise."

"It's a deal," Elizabeth told her. "Meanwhile, I'll do an Internet search on gemstone marbles, and see what I can come up with."

The girls were almost home, and Elizabeth could see her parents' van parked in the driveway. She looked at her watch—7:25. *It must have been a short meeting.*

"I'll see you tomorrow, Beth," Megan called as she headed toward her front door. "Join me on my break again tomorrow. We can talk about what you find on the Internet!"

"See you then," Elizabeth called back, and climbed the front steps.

•—•—•

Later that night, Elizabeth sat at the family computer searching for information on the marbles. Her mother put the finishing touches on the now gleaming kitchen, and laid a fresh dish towel on the counter.

"What are you looking at?" Mrs. Anderson asked, laying a gentle hand on Elizabeth's shoulder.

"Oh, I'm just helping Megan with a project. Do you need the computer?" Elizabeth asked her mother.

"No, I'm going to bed now. Don't stay up too late, okay?" She kissed her daughter on the cheek and headed toward the back of the house. Then, she called over her shoulder, "Your dad will be home in a little while, though, and you know he'll want to check his e-mail."

Elizabeth laughed. Her father taught Bible classes at the local seminary. He often got e-mails from his students, asking about their assignments. He enjoyed his job, and he loved helping his students understand the Bible better. To him, that was as exciting as a carnival would have been for Elizabeth.

She typed into the search engine, *Precious gemstone marbles*, and waited to see what appeared. Before long, she had links to museums and fine jewelers all over the world. There was a link for birthstone marbles, precious gemstones, forever gemstones, tigereye marbles. . .but nothing related to Amarillo, Texas.

If only I could send an SOS to the Camp Club Girls. Elizabeth thought of her friends from summer camp. *But I promised Jean Louise I'd keep my mouth shut.* She was in the middle of another search when a flag popped up in the bottom corner of her screen. HORSEGIRL96 WANTS TO CHAT the message read.

Elizabeth recognized McKenzie's online name and clicked on the flag.

Did you get my letter? McKenzie typed.

Elizabeth: *Yes! I'm so excited!*

McKenzie: *Me too. I can't wait to see you.*

Elizabeth: *What day will you be here?*

McKenzie: *Next Tuesday.*

Elizabeth smiled. She couldn't wait to see her friend. Then, she had an idea.

Elizabeth: *Do you think your parents will let you stay at my house while you're here?*

McKenzie: *That sounds like fun! I'll ask and e-mail you tomorrow. Maybe you can stay at the hotel with me some, too.*

Elizabeth: *Okay, I'll ask. Talk to you later.*

McKenzie: *Bye.*

Elizabeth was smiling at the computer screen when her dad walked in. "Hey, Bethy-bug! What are you so happy about?"

She stood and hugged her father. "Hi, Daddy! Guess what? McKenzie's coming to visit. She and her family will be in Amarillo next Tuesday!"

"That's great news, Sparky," he said, using one of his many pet names for her. "Why don't you see if she can sleep over while she's in town?"

Elizabeth giggled. "I already asked her. She's supposed to let me know tomorrow."

Mr. Anderson walked over to the computer and sat down. "What's all this about gemstones you've pulled up?"

Elizabeth had to think quickly. She didn't want to break her promise, but she wasn't going to lie, either. "Oh, just some research I'm doing for Megan."

"You're a good friend, Elizabeth, and an all-around

great gal. Just like your mama. 'A wife of noble character who can find? She is worth far more than rubies,' Proverbs 31:10. Tell Megan the real gem is your mama," he said.

Elizabeth smiled. Her parents were kind of sappy sometimes, always holding hands and kissing. It was embarrassing at times, but it was cute.

"I'll tell her, Daddy," she said, and kissed him on top of his head. "Good night."

•—•—•

At 2:33 p.m. the next day, Elizabeth pushed open the saloon-style doors of the Big Texan Steak Ranch and looked around. Megan was already sitting at her table. Two tall iced drinks and two big slices of pie were there, too.

Elizabeth tossed her blond hair over her shoulders as she slid into the booth. Megan looked worn-out.

"I don't know how long I can keep this up!" she moaned. "I'm not sure I was created for hard physical labor."

Elizabeth chuckled. She remembered how tired she had been at camp, after she and her friends had to do kitchen duty for a few days. "You can do it. Hang in there," she encouraged.

Megan leaned forward. "So, did you find out anything about the marbles?" she whispered.

"Not a thing. I did an Internet search, but nothing linked any gemstone marbles to Amarillo. I didn't have time to look at much. I'll keep trying."

"Why don't you get all your Camp Detective Club Friends, or whatever y'all called yourselves, to help?" Megan asked.

"Camp Club Girls," Elizabeth corrected. "I thought about that, but we promised Jean Louise to keep it hush-hush."

"Well, we don't need to talk about it to people around here. But as long as you trust your friends, I trust them."

Elizabeth sighed with relief. This would be so much easier if her friends helped her. "Okay," she said. "I'll send out an e-mail tonight, and we'll see what we can come up with. You're still going to talk to your mom tonight, aren't you?"

"I hope so. As much as she's been working lately, I hardly see her. And when I do see her, she can barely stand up, she's so tired. I'm not sure how to break it to her that her mother lost her marbles," she said.

Elizabeth giggled and thought about the situation. It sure would be nice if Megan's mom didn't have to work so hard. Her dad had been killed a few years ago in a car accident, and things had been tough for their family since then. "I don't know about you, but I'm about to die if I don't start eating this pie! What is it today? Chocolate?" she asked.

"I think so," said Megan without much enthusiasm. But then she took a bite, and perked up right away. "Oh, this is *so* good!"

"I wonder if they'd hire me and let me work for pie,"

Elizabeth said. Both girls giggled and finished their pie in no time.

Just then, Jean Louise stopped by the table and bent down to their level. "You girls had better get crackin' on that marble mystery. That man was snooping around here again this morning, asking more questions."

The two girls looked at each other in surprise. Yes, they definitely needed to get crackin'.

•—•—•

Elizabeth typed into the subject line of the e-mail: NEW MYSTERY; NEED HELP! She then moved her cursor to the body of the e-mail, and began typing the whole story. She ended it with, "I don't know where to begin. Please help!"

She paused and said a little prayer before hitting the SEND button. *Lord, you know Megan and her mother haven't had an easy life. These gemstones could really help them. Please help us find them.*

There. She sent the e-mail and sat staring at the blank screen. She knew it would only be a matter of minutes before someone answered her.

Since summer camp had ended, the six Camp Club Girls had conspired to solve several mysteries. Elizabeth had traveled to DC and helped her friend Sydney uncover a plot to assassinate the president! The other girls had been busy as well, using the sleuthing skills they had honed at camp to solve their own hometown mysteries. They were becoming quite the team, and Elizabeth knew she could count on them to offer helpful suggestions in this new case. The miracles of e-mail, text messaging, and Internet research had allowed them to keep in close contact, from Alex in California to Sydney in Washington, DC. Sure enough, just minutes after she sent her message, the red flag popped up. It was Bailey.

> *Gemstones? How exciting! Your friend will be rich! Wow, I wish I were there. You should check the local jewelers and see if anyone in your area sells gemstone marbles.*

Elizabeth smiled. She missed Bailey, the youngest of their gang. Bailey was always excited about everything. Period.

Elizabeth typed back, *Great idea. Thanks, Bales!*

Just then, another red flag showed that Alexis was online.

> *Why doesn't your friend snoop around the restaurant and see if there are any hiding places there? She can act like she's cleaning or something. Tell her to try tapping on the walls. Nancy Drew is always tapping on walls to see if they are hollow.*

A third red flag popped up, and it was Sydney.

Sounds to me like you need to investigate Megan's grandmother's death. It's suspicious to me that she died just days after receiving the jewels.

Elizabeth felt her heart beating faster. This was getting more and more exciting. She typed the words, *Thanks, y'all. This will really help me get started. I'll keep you posted.*

She signed off the computer and walked to the front porch. She would wait there until Megan got home.

•—•—•

An hour later, the two girls sat on Elizabeth's front steps sipping the fresh lemonade Mrs. Anderson had brought out to them. "How much do you know about your grandmother's death?" asked Elizabeth. She had already shared the suggestions she'd received from her friends.

"Only that it was an accident. She was hit by a car."

"Are you sure it was an accident?" Elizabeth prodded.

Megan gave her an exasperated look. "I don't know, Elizabeth. I wasn't there."

Elizabeth giggled. "Oh, yeah. Sorry. But how can we find out more?"

"We can ask my mom. But she doesn't like to talk about it. She loves talking about her mother. But when it comes to talking about her death, she clams up."

"What about Jean Louise?" Elizabeth asked. "She knew your grandmother. Maybe she can tell us more."

Megan's face brightened. "That's a great idea! Why didn't I think of that?"

"Because you're not an experienced detective, like I am," Elizabeth teased.

They heard the phone ring, and a moment later Elizabeth's mother called out, "Elizabeth, it's for you! It's your friend McKenzie calling, so hurry!"

Elizabeth went into the house, but Megan kept her seat.

"Hello? McKenzie?" Elizabeth spoke excitedly into the phone.

"It's me! I've been working outside, and I just now checked my e-mail. I asked my parents, and the answer is yes! I can stay with you some while we're there. But they said if it's okay with you and your parents, you can stay some with me at the motel. We're staying at the Big Texan, because of their horse hotel. Isn't that cool, a horse hotel?"

"McKenzie, that's perfect! Did you read my other e-mail?"

"I just skimmed it. I was so excited about staying with you, I went straight to ask my parents, and then I called you. I figured you could fill me in on the phone."

"Well, Megan works at the Big Texan Steak Ranch! That is the same restaurant her grandmother worked at, when she got the marbles. We may want to stay at the Big Texan as much as possible, so we can snoop around."

"Oh, this will be awesome! I was already excited about seeing you, but now we'll get to solve a mystery while I'm there! I can't wait," she gushed into the phone.

The girls said their good-byes with promises to e-mail later in the evening. Then, Elizabeth returned to the porch.

"Guess what?" she asked Megan.

"Uhmmm, let me guess. McKenzie and her family are staying at the Big Texan, and you'll stay with her while she's here."

Elizabeth grinned. "I guess I did talk kind of loud. But I'm excited! I still have to ask my parents, though."

Just then, Megan's mom pulled into the driveway. She cleaned houses in the wealthy part of town. She also cleaned rooms for several local hotels, including The Big Texan.

"Are you going to tell her what's going on?" Elizabeth asked.

"I guess it's now or never," said Megan. "Why don't you come with me? You can fix Mama some pie and iced tea while I break the news."

The Charming Stranger

The girls walked across the driveway, and Megan hugged her mother. The woman's hair was falling out of its pretty clasp, and she had tired circles under her eyes. Still, she was beautiful.

Before Megan's parents had met, Ruby Smith had been Miss Amarillo. As small children, Elizabeth and Megan had enjoyed hiding under her bed and watching her experiment with different hairstyles or shades of lipstick. Once, she had fixed her hair in crazy crooked braids, and put cold cream all over her face. Then, she had said in a loud voice, "I think I'm ready. I sure wish Megan and Elizabeth were here to tell me how I look!"

The girls had burst into a fit of giggles. Mrs. Smith had coaxed them from under the bed and given them makeovers. But now, things were different. She didn't even wear makeup any more.

"Hi, girls," she said, offering an exhausted smile. "How are y'all today?"

"We're great, Mama," Megan responded. "Here, let me

carry your bag. Come on in and sit down. I need to talk to you."

Elizabeth followed them into the house and walked into the kitchen. She felt as comfortable here as she did in her own kitchen. Pulling three glasses out of the cabinet, she filled them with ice. She figured she'd let Megan and her mom have some privacy.

She poured sweet tea from a pitcher in the refrigerator and transferred three slices of chocolate pie from the box to small plates. She found forks and napkins. Then she listened to see if Megan had told her mother the news yet.

"Megan, what are you talking about?" Mrs. Smith asked her.

"Mom, I'm telling you, we're rich! We just don't know where our treasure is."

" 'For where your treasure is, there your heart will be also,' " Mrs. Smith quoted Matthew 6:21.

Megan paused. "Mom, this is serious. Some man gave Grandma some priceless gemstone marbles. We have to find out what happened to them!"

Though Megan had never met her grandmother, she still referred to her as "Grandma." She told Elizabeth once that she liked imagining what the woman was like.

Mrs. Smith yawned. "Elizabeth, what's taking you so long, child? I thought you were fixin' us some tea!"

Elizabeth appeared with the tea tray.

"Look at you!" the woman smiled. "Before ya' know it, you'll be working at the restaurant with Megan. How did you girls grow up so fast?"

Megan looked frustrated. Her mother clearly didn't understand how important the gemstones were. "Mom, aren't you going to try to find out more about the marbles?"

Mrs. Smith took a bite of her pie and then leaned back. "Megan, honey, that sounds like a wonderful story. But if any lost jewels existed, we would have heard about them long before now. If this little story makes you happy, and you want to go hunting these marbles, go right ahead. I'm tired, and I don't have room in my life right now for fairy tales." Then, seeing Megan's disappointed look, she sighed. "I'll tell you what. I'll call your Uncle Jack and see if he knows anything. I was only nine, but he was fifteen. Maybe he remembers something I don't. But then I don't want to hear any more about it. I—I don't like to think about that time."

Megan leaned over her mother's chair, hugged her, and then sat back down. The three finished their pie and tea, and Elizabeth excused herself. "Thank you for the refreshments. I'd better get home now. I'll see you tomorrow, Megan."

Megan waved good-bye, and Elizabeth let herself out. She could tell her friend was disappointed. But Mrs. Smith's disinterest might not be a bad thing. The woman had experienced a lot of discouragement in her life. It might be better not to get her hopes up.

" 'Those who hope in the Lord will renew their strength.' " Elizabeth thought of the verse she had known for years. *Lord,* she prayed, *Mrs. Smith could use some hope and some strength. Please help us find those jewels.*

•—•—•

The next couple of days passed quickly as Elizabeth continued to research the gemstones. She found several more dealers, but nothing about stolen or missing marbles. She was glad when Tuesday rolled around, and sat waiting by the phone. McKenzie was supposed to call when she arrived at The Big Texan Motel.

Elizabeth jumped when the phone finally rang. "Hello?"

"Beth, it's Mac. We're here!"

Elizabeth squealed. "I'll be there in ten minutes!" she told her friend, and nearly hung up before she asked for the room number.

"I'm in room thirty-four, right in front of this big, funny shaped pool," McKenzie told her.

Elizabeth stopped in her tracks. "Mac, surely you know that pool is in the shape of Texas."

McKenzie giggled. "I know. I just wanted to hear what you'd say to me. I've heard you Texans are very proud of your state."

"It's only the best place on God's green earth!" Elizabeth said.

"Well, that may be true, but I haven't seen much green yet. You didn't tell me you live in the desert!" McKenzie teased.

Elizabeth laughed. "I'll see you in ten—no, in five minutes!"

She kissed her mother on the cheek. Mom had invited Mac and her family for dinner, and was planning to stop by the motel later to introduce herself.

Elizabeth was almost out the door when James called, "I want to come!"

"That's not a bad idea," Mrs. Anderson said. "Elizabeth, James has been cooped up in this house all day. Would you take him with you? I'll be there in less than thirty minutes to get him."

Elizabeth sighed. "Come on, little brother."

James lunged at her, squeezing her. "Thank you, Bettyboo! You are the best sister in the world."

Elizabeth hugged him back, and said, "You won't think that if you keep calling me Bettyboo!"

James giggled and ran out the door ahead of her. "Bettyboo, Bettyboo, Bettyboo!"

Elizabeth took off after him. Some days she didn't know whether to hug her little brother, or clobber him.

An hour later, she and McKenzie sat by the large, Texas-shaped pool sipping sodas, while Mrs. Anderson visited with Mr. and Mrs. Phillips. James and McKenzie's eight-year-old brother, Evan, sat on the edge of the pool splashing their feet in the water and using a paper cup as a boat.

"So, when do I get to meet Megan?" Mac asked. "Is there any more news on the marbles?"

"We'll walk down to the restaurant in a few minutes. Her break isn't for another half hour. We've hit a dead end with the marbles. Her mother just isn't interested in finding out about them. She thinks it's a fairy tale."

McKenzie thought about that. "I guess she doesn't remember anything about the man or the marbles. I wonder if there is anybody else we can ask."

"I guess we can talk to Jean Louise some more, but I think she's told us all she knows," said Elizabeth.

The two girls leaned back in their lounge chairs, sipped their drinks, and thought about the mystery.

•—•—•

A little while later, the girls pushed open the doors of the restaurant and adjusted their vision.

"Well, look who's here!" Jean Louise greeted them in her nasal twang. "You must be here to see Megs. I think her usual table is open, and she'll be out in a few."

"Megs?" McKenzie whispered as they walked through the restaurant.

"That's Jean Louise. Megs is a pet name for Megan. Watch out. She has a pet name for everyone, and I'm sure she'll come up with something for you, too."

McKenzie smiled. "What does she call you?"

After a pause, Elizabeth giggled. "Liza Jane. She sings a song about 'Li'l Liza Jane' to me."

Just then, Megan slid into the booth next to Elizabeth. "Hi! You must be McKenzie." She reached out her hand.

McKenzie returned the handshake. "And you must be Megan."

They were interrupted by Jean Louise, smacking her gum. "I see you've added a new person to your club," she said. "How ya' doin', Red?"

McKenzie smiled at the reference to her hair.

"McKenzie and Elizabeth are experienced mystery-solvers. They're going to help me find out about the—" Megan started to say.

"Shhhh!" Jean Louise snapped. She leaned forward. "I thought I told you to keep this quiet."

McKenzie looked confused.

Megan told her, "It's okay, Jean Louise. McKenzie is Elizabeth's friend, and I trust her. Besides, she's not from around here. She'll be gone in a few days."

Jean Louise eyed Mac with suspicion, but then her gaze softened. "Well, what's done is done. But you need to hush up. The man who has been nosing around is sitting right over there."

The three girls turned, trying to get a look at the man

in the cowboy boots. His long legs stuck awkwardly from under the table, and he looked a bit like a giant at a tea party.

"Turn around!" Jean Louise whispered. "I thought you girls were supposed to be detectives. You don't want him to know you're staring at him!"

The girls whipped back around in their seats. "Oh, yeah, she's right," said Mac. "Elizabeth, you have the best angle. Tell us what you see."

"Well, uh, he looks about my dad's age, and he's having a cheeseburger and french fries," she said.

"Who cares what he's eating?" Megan whispered.

Jean Louise rolled her eyes. "Look, girls, why don't you wait until he gets up to leave. Then you can get a better look. For now, just hold your horses. I'll bring you some leftover pecan pie." She turned to leave.

"Jean Louise," called Elizabeth.

The woman turned back around, and Elizabeth continued. "Is there any more you can tell us, or anyone else we can talk to?"

Jean Louise cocked one hip and rested her notepad there. "I've told you girls all I know, and nobody else was around back then, except my—hey! Why don't I take you girls to meet my mama? She would love the company, and Megan, she would just love to meet you. She loved your grandma so much. It nearly broke her heart when she died."

The girls perked up at the idea. "That sounds great," Megan answered. "When can we go?"

"You're off tomorrow, aren't you? Why don't we go about ten o'clock in the morning. Meet me here, and I'll drive you over." She looked at the other two girls. "Since y'all are in on this too, you're welcome to come if your parents agree." With that, the woman moved to another table to refill some iced tea glasses.

Elizabeth continued to discreetly eye the cowboy. "That is one tall man," she said. "Did y'all see how long his legs are?"

Just then, the man looked directly at Elizabeth and smiled. Had he heard her? She quickly looked away, then back. He winked at her!

She could feel the heat rising to her cheeks. Then she giggled.

"What? What are you laughing at?" the other two asked her.

"He winked at me!" she whispered. They all leaned to look at the man, who was now walking toward the cash register. His head nearly brushed against the ceiling fans, and he had to duck around the longhorn chandeliers.

"Let's follow him," Mac whispered. She and Elizabeth stood to leave.

"Wait! I'm not through with my shift!" Megan called.

Just then, Jean Louise showed up with their pie. "You're not leaving before you have this, are you?"

Elizabeth and McKenzie looked at each other, then at the man. "Can you put it in a box for us? We'll be back for it later!" Elizabeth told her, and they followed the man. "Thanks, Jean Louise!" she called over her shoulder.

Megan and Jean Louise stared open-mouthed after the two girls. "Apparently, they're serious about this detective business," said Megan.

Out in the sunlight, the girls looked to the right and the left. They barely caught sight of the tall man in the cowboy hat as he turned the corner. They followed quickly, trying to act casual.

As they turned the corner, they crashed into James. Mrs. Anderson was a few steps behind him.

"Beth! McKenzie's daddy is going to let me ride a horse! Mama's taking me home now to get my boots and cowboy hat!"

Elizabeth and McKenzie peered over Mrs. Anderson's shoulder at the tall man. He was going, going. . .gone.

"I thought you two were going to sit with Megan during her break. That was a short break," the woman said.

"Well, we. . .uh," Elizabeth stammered.

James jumped up and down. "Do ya' want to ride horses with me, Beth?"

McKenzie jumped in. "That will be fun, James. We'll meet you at the stables in a little while."

Mrs. Anderson and James waved and continued toward

the parking lot. The girls went in the opposite direction, trying to determine where the man had turned.

"He could have turned here, at the ice machines, or up there, or. . .it's no use. We lost him," Elizabeth said.

"Well, since he walked toward the rooms, he's probably a guest here. Maybe we should hang out here today and see if he turns up again," McKenzie replied.

"Sounds like a plan to me."

•—•—•

Later that afternoon, the two Camp Club Girls leaned on the railing of the Big Texan Horse Hotel. Evan waited patiently as Mr. Phillips led James, dressed in red hat and boots, on a black-and-white spotted pony. "Giddy-up! Look, Beth! I'm a cowboy!"

McKenzie laughed. "Your brother sure is cute!"

Elizabeth smiled. "Yeah, I guess he's okay, as far as brothers go." She waved at James as he rode by.

Sue Anderson and Jen Phillips sat on a long bench in the shade, talking.

Elizabeth continued, "I can't wait for you to meet my dad."

"Aren't we all going to your house for dinner tonight?" McKenzie questioned.

"That's the plan. Dad's going to cook out. We'll have hamburgers and hot dogs. Mom even got a watermelon."

"Yummm! I love watermelon," McKenzie continued. They both waved at James again. Neither noticed the tall shadow that appeared beside them until Mr. Phillips looked up and smiled.

"You've got a couple of mighty fine lookin' cowboys there," said the man, gesturing to Evan and James.

"Yep. Cowboys in training, anyway," said Mr. Phillips, helping James down from the pony. When both boys were safely out of the paddock, McKenzie's dad held out his hand. "Dan Phillips," he said.

"I'm Mark Jacobs," said the man, and the two shook hands.

"Is one of these horses yours?" asked Mr. Phillips.

The man pointed to a gorgeous brown and white quarterhorse. "That's Lucy. She's one of the best horses I've ever owned. I'm going to miss her."

"You're getting rid of her?" Phillips asked.

"Yep. I'm here for the rodeo this weekend. I'm riding in it. But this rodeo life is getting tiresome, and I'm looking to retire. I want to buy a little spread of land about ten miles from here, but I need to sell all my stock to do it. I'm also waiting for a few other things to fall into place."

Elizabeth and McKenzie looked at one another, wide-eyed.

Phillips looked at Lucy. "Would she be any good on a ranch?" he asked.

"Oh, definitely. She was bred for ranching. Like I said, she's one of the best horses I've worked with," the man said.

"I've been looking to buy another horse for my ranch.

We live in Montana. I may be interested in buying her when you finally get ready to sell. Of course, I'd like to see her in action," Mr. Phillips told him.

"Why don't you come watch the rodeo tomorrow night? Bring your whole family. I have a box reserved, but nobody to fill it," the man said.

Elizabeth and McKenzie made frantic eye contact but remained quiet.

Mr. Phillips and Mr. Jacobs began walking toward where the two women sat in the shade. Mr. Phillips introduced the ladies, then told them, "Mark, here, has invited us to be his guests at the rodeo."

"All of you," Mr. Jacobs said, looking at Elizabeth's mom. "Bring your families. I've got about a dozen seats just waiting to be filled."

"That is very kind of you," Mrs. Anderson replied. "Why don't you join us at our house this evening? We're having a cookout. When Robert, my husband, starts grilling, he goes a little overboard, and we usually have enough food to feed an army!"

Jacobs laughed. "He sounds like my kind of man. I'd love to join you. I'm on the road most of the time, and I don't get many home-cooked meals."

Elizabeth didn't know if this was a good development or a bad one.

Mr. Phillips noticed the girls and motioned to them.

"Girls, this is Mr. Jacobs. Mark, this is my daughter McKenzie and her friend Elizabeth."

"I. . .uh. . .it's a pleasure to meet you, sir." Elizabeth held out her hand. McKenzie followed suit.

"I believe I saw these young ladies at the restaurant." The man smiled.

The men turned toward the bench where the two women were seated and continued their conversation.

"What are we going to do?" McKenzie whispered.

"What do you mean?" Elizabeth whispered back.

"Well, this man clearly is a crook. I can't let my dad do business with him! And we certainly don't want him coming to your house!"

"What makes you think he's a crook?" Elizabeth asked, though she had the same idea about the man.

"Just look at him! He's way too handsome to be honest," McKenzie whispered frantically. "Look at that smile. He's just oozing with charm. That can't be real."

The girls stared at the tall, good-looking cowboy who looked like he had just ridden into town straight from a movie set. At that moment, the man turned and saw them looking at him. He winked!

A Peek into the Past

Elizabeth and McKenzie looked at one another in shock, but remained quiet. They weren't sure what to make of this development.

Mrs. Anderson smiled. "It's settled then. You can come over with the Phillips family. We'll see you all around seven?"

The adults agreed to the time, and Elizabeth's mother stood to leave. "I'd better get going, so I can prepare our feast! Elizabeth, are you coming home with me, or would you like to stay awhile longer?"

"Oh, I'll stay here if that's okay. McKenzie and I really need to talk to Megan."

Mrs. Anderson looked at her. "You're not distracting Megan from her work, are you? I wouldn't want her to get in trouble."

"No, ma'am. That's why we're waiting here until she gets off."

"Well, be sure to invite Megan and her mother for dinner," Mrs. Anderson said. She took James by the hand and bid the group good-bye.

The two girls walked casually around the stables, pretending to look at horses.

"What should we do?" asked McKenzie.

"I think we should stay close, and see what happens," said Elizabeth.

"But now he's coming to your house! He'll know where you live!" McKenzie continued.

"So?" Elizabeth said.

"So, I just don't like the idea of the man we're trying to investigate getting so close to you and your family," McKenzie told her.

"Look," Elizabeth said. "We don't have any reason to believe he's dangerous. We only think he knows something about the gemstones. I think we should just play dumb, and see if he brings up the marbles."

After a moment, McKenzie nodded. "Okay. But this feels strange to me."

The two girls stopped a few steps from the stall where the cowboy and McKenzie's dad were talking horse talk.

"McKenzie, here, is a horse expert in her own right," her dad said, inviting the girls into the conversation.

McKenzie blushed and smiled. "I try," she said modestly.

"She'll take over the ranch for me one day, if she wants," her dad smiled proudly at her. "She could probably do it right now."

The cowboy smiled. "It's always good to have someone

around who knows their business," he said. Then, he reached out and shook Mr. Phillips's hand and tipped his hat to the girls. "I have some other business I need to tend to, but I'll look forward to seeing you all at dinner," he said. And with that, his long, lanky legs carried him across the stables, around the corner, and out of sight.

•—•—•

The girls spent the next couple of hours sitting by the pool and looking at the different horses. Elizabeth enjoyed seeing the Big Texan from a tourist's point of view. She had lived in Amarillo all her life and had never stayed at the motel. It was fun.

At 4:00 p.m., they went to the motel lobby. McKenzie had noticed a computer available to the motel guests. They wanted to check their e-mail and see if there were any more tips from the other Camp Club Girls. After waiting for two other people, they signed on.

Sure enough, there was a message from Kate.

Biscuit was sniffing around in the car today, and he found my reader pen! I've been looking all over for that thing. But it got me thinking. . . I wonder if Emily Marie hid the marbles in her car somewhere.

What happened to her car after she died?

"That's a good question. Let's go ask Megan. If she doesn't know, maybe Jean Louise will know something," suggested Elizabeth.

They headed to the restaurant. Megan wasn't scheduled to get off until 4:30, but they were hoping to eat their forgotten pie while they waited. Jean Louise met them at the door.

"Well, well. If it isn't Sherlock Holmes and Watson," she said with a smile. "Did you track down the cowboy?"

The girls laughed. "Actually, he found us," Elizabeth told her. "It's been an interesting afternoon."

Jean Louise seated them, then brought their pie, all nestled in white, Styrofoam containers. "Here ya go," she said. The restaurant was busy, and she didn't stay to chat.

Twenty minutes later, Megan joined them at the booth. "Tell me everything," she said.

"We will. But first, do you have any idea what happened to your grandmother's car after she died?"

Megan thought for a moment. "No, but my Uncle Jack will know. He's a mechanic, and Mom says he's always been interested in cars."

"Let's go see him right now!" exclaimed McKenzie.

"That will be hard. He lives in Houston," Megan said. "But I can call him."

The girls leaned their heads together, whispering and planning for the next half hour.

•—•—•

That evening, Elizabeth's backyard was filled with laughter and the scent of grilling hamburgers. James and Evan ran around playing cowboys and Indians, and Mr. Jacobs pretended to get shot in the crossfire. The man seemed to enjoy children, and moved back and forth between playing with the boys and helping Mr. Anderson flip burgers.

Elizabeth was inside filling red plastic cups with iced tea. She had left McKenzie sitting near the men in case anything was said about the jewels. She looked out the window at her friend, who looked bored. The last bit of conversation Elizabeth had heard was about football.

"You did invite Megan and her mom, didn't you?" Mrs. Anderson asked Elizabeth.

"Yes, ma'am. Megan said her mom gets home tonight around seven thirty, so they'll be a little late."

Mrs. Anderson looked out the side window toward the Smiths' house. "I sure wish she didn't have to work so hard. I wish we could do something more for them," she said.

"We're actually working on that," said Elizabeth without thinking.

"What do you mean?" her mother asked.

Catching herself, Elizabeth thought quickly. "Oh, just that Megan is working now, earning some extra money. She also makes straight A's in school, and in a few years she'll probably get a full scholarship to some college."

Mrs. Anderson ran a gentle hand across Elizabeth's hair. "That's nice, dear." Then, the woman held open the screen door with her backside, and the two joined the party, delivering iced tea to their guests.

A short time later, Megan arrived with her mother. When Mrs. Smith was introduced to Mr. Jacobs, the cowboy stood and took her hand. "It's a pleasure to meet you, Ruby. You add a whole new loveliness to your name," he said.

Mrs. Smith smiled and blushed, and the three girls looked at one another in alarm. What did that cowboy think he was doing? Did he know about the jewels and Megan's mother?

They continued to watch the interaction between Ruby and Mr. Jacobs throughout the evening. Those two didn't talk much, but their eyes kept wandering to each other. Finally, Megan whispered, "We need to have an emergency meeting in your room. Now!"

The three girls excused themselves. As soon as Elizabeth's door was closed, Megan burst into a chain of broken sentences that showed her anxiety, but didn't really make much sense.

"What in the—who does he think—and my mother! I've never seen her—she used to flirt with my dad but—of all people! I've wanted her to start dating—but not like this! Not with that no good, sweet-talkin', connivin', manipulatin' cowboy!"

"Whoa, calm down, Megs." Elizabeth put her arm around her friend. "She's not dating anyone. Sure, there were some sparks out there. But let's face it. She'll probably never see him again after tonight. Unless. . ."

"Unless what?" Megan and McKenzie asked in unison.

Elizabeth paused. If the looks on their faces were any indication, her two friends were thinking exactly what she was thinking. "Unless he knows the jewels were given to your grandmother. Do you think he's traced them to your mother somehow?"

"How could he? My mother didn't know about them until the other day. And she doesn't even care about them."

"She may not care about them, but he doesn't know that," said McKenzie.

The three girls moved Elizabeth's pink ruffled curtains to the side and peered at the group in the backyard. Cowboy had moved his lawn chair closer to Megan's mother, and the two looked engrossed in conversation.

"We'd better get out there. Now!" exclaimed Megan.

"Not just yet," McKenzie interrupted. "First, tell us if you had a chance to call your uncle."

Megan kept peering out the window as she answered. "Oh, yeah. I called him this afternoon. He doesn't know anything about any marbles. He said the car stayed impounded for a couple of years while they investigated the accident. After that, he took it apart and sold it piece by piece. They needed the money. But if there were any marbles hidden in the car, he would have found them."

McKenzie let out a disappointed sigh. "I was just sure that's where they were."

The sound of Mrs. Smith's laughter floated through the window, and Megan said, "That does it. I've gotta get that cowboy away from my mother."

"Yep. And we'd better get crackin' on this mystery, before your mother really gets hurt," said Elizabeth.

•—•—•

The cookout ended around 10:30, but had seemed much longer. The girls did all they could to interrupt the conversations between Megan's mom and the cowboy, but the man was not easily deterred. This gave the three sleuths even more reason to think he was up to something shady.

They spent the night in Elizabeth's room and were awakened early the next morning with the sounds of humming from Megan's driveway. Megan sat up in her sleeping bag and peered out the window to see her mother leaving for work.

"My mother hasn't sounded like that in a long time," she said.

Elizabeth rolled over and propped her head on her elbow. "She really misses your dad, doesn't she?"

"Yeah," Megan answered softly. "So do I."

They were interrupted by James. "Who wants

breakfast?" he asked, opening the door without knocking.

Elizabeth squealed, "Shut the door! James, you know you're not allowed in here without permission!"

He backed out and shut the door. "Sorry, Beth. But Mama wants to know who wants breakfast."

"I do," called all three girls in unison.

"Little brothers. . . ," muttered Elizabeth, and her friends chuckled. The three girls dressed quickly and dashed to the kitchen, where Mrs. Anderson had left toaster pastries, fruit, orange juice, and milk. James had already eaten, so they had the kitchen to themselves.

"We're supposed to meet Jean Louise at the restaurant at nine forty-five so she can drive us to her mother's house. Did you check with your mom, Elizabeth?" asked Megan.

"Mom," called Elizabeth around a mouthful of toaster pastry.

Mrs. Anderson popped her head around the corner from the laundry room. "Don't talk with your mouth full, dear."

Elizabeth swallowed her food and wiped her mouth with her napkin. "Sorry. May I please go with Jean Louise this morning to meet her mother? Megan's coming, too, and McKenzie is going to ask her parents."

Mrs. Anderson smiled. "I think that sounds lovely. I'm glad to hear you girls are doing something constructive with your time. It reminds me of James 1:27."

Megan and McKenzie looked at Elizabeth after Mrs. Anderson went back to her laundry. "James 1:27?" Megan asked.

" 'Religion that God our Father accepts as pure and faultless is this: to look after orphans and widows in their distress and to keep oneself from being polluted by the world,' " Elizabeth quoted.

The other two listened in stunned silence. "How do you do that?" asked McKenzie. "I know a lot of Bible verses, but you're like a walking encyclopedia!"

Elizabeth smiled. "I don't know. I've just heard them all my life."

"Well, we're not exactly going to see this woman because she's in distress," said Megan. "So I'm not sure this visit will count."

"Maybe not, but I'll bet she'll enjoy our visit anyway! Hopefully, we'll get some information we can use," replied Elizabeth. "We've got to find those jewels before the cowboy does."

A short time later, having gained permission from McKenzie's parents, the three girls slid into Jean Louise's red convertible sports car.

"This is a cool car!" McKenzie exclaimed.

"Thank you," said the waitress.

The girls enjoyed the ride, laughing as their hair—blond, brunette, and auburn—flapped in the wind.

They arrived at Shady Acres Retirement Community a short time later, and Jean Louise led them through the well-kept apartment complex. She knocked and then used her key to open the door. "Mama!" she called. "We're here. I brought the girls I told you about."

A small, white-haired woman appeared, using a walker. Her eyes were bright, and she wore a cheerful smile. "Come in, come in!" she said. "I've been looking forward to this."

They entered the small, well-kept apartment, and smelled something delicious. Jean Louise wasted no time in introducing the girls, one by one. "And this, ladies, is my mother, Mrs. Wilson."

"It's a pleasure to meet you, Mrs. Wilson," the girls said politely.

"Sit down," she gestured, and moved slowly to stand in front of Megan. "Except you. I want you to stand here and let me look at you."

Megan smiled a bit uncomfortably while the woman looked her over, head to toe. Then, she reached out a gentle hand and touched Megan's hair, then her face. "Such a beautiful girl. You're the spitting image of Emily Marie."

McKenzie looked questioningly at Elizabeth.

"Megan's grandmother," Elizabeth whispered, and the redhead nodded.

"Your grandmother would have been so proud of you," the woman continued. "She was my best friend, you know.

A real jewel. Your mother and your uncle Jack were her world. She would have loved watching you grow up."

Then, she gestured for Megan to sit down before taking a seat herself. She turned to her daughter. "Jean Louise, I made some lemon bars for these girls, and there is lemonade in the refrigerator. Would you get them, please?"

"Yes, ma'am." The woman moved swiftly to obey her elderly mother.

"I hope you didn't go to any trouble, Mrs. Wilson," Elizabeth said.

The woman responded by waving her hand in the air, as if any such talk was nonsense. Elizabeth liked this woman.

"I understand you have some questions for me," she said, keeping her eyes on Megan.

"Yes, ma'am," Megan said. "Jean Louise told us about some marbles, but I don't know anything about them, and neither does my mother."

The woman smiled. "Oh, the marbles. I remember that day so well. Emily Marie came walking into the break room at the restaurant, white as a sheet. She closed the door, and it was just the two of us. Then, she pulled out a little white cloth sack, and poured out the contents on the table in front of me. They were marbles, and they were the prettiest things I had ever seen."

She paused, as if remembering, then continued. " 'They're real,' she told me.

" 'Real marbles?' I asked. I was confused. Of course they were real marbles.

" 'Real gemstones,' she said, and plopped down in front of me. 'Foster gave them to me.'

"Now, Foster was the tall, handsome cowboy who had taken a shine to Emily Marie. He wasn't from around here, but he came through town a lot on business. He began to have more and more business in Amarillo, but no one was fooled. He came to town to see your grandma. She was a beautiful woman." Mrs. Wilson pushed her hair back from her face.

"I was speechless. I had never seen anything like the marbles in front of me. I picked up the emerald and held it up to the light. Then, we both started giggling like school girls."

Elizabeth smiled at the image.

The woman paused as Jean Louise brought in the refreshments and placed them on the coffee table. "Keep going, Mama. Don't stop on my account," Jean Louise said.

The woman leaned back in her chair with a smile. "After our giggles were under control, I held up the ruby. 'Won't this make a nice gift for your little Ruby, one day?' I asked her.

"She looked at me like I'd gone crazy. 'I can't keep them!' she said.

" 'Why in the world not?' I asked her.

" 'It's too much. It would be different if Foster and I

were engaged, but we're not.'

" 'Oh, you will be,' I told her. 'I've seen the way he looks at you. And I've seen the way you look at him. You'll be married before the year is out.'

"When I said that, Emily blushed four shades of red. But she was smiling. 'Maybe so,' she said.

" 'Besides,' I told her. 'You can't give them back. He'll think you're rejecting him.'

"She sat quietly, looking at those jewels long after my break was over. I covered for her for a while. I knew she needed some time to think. Finally, she joined me back on the floor, waiting tables like nothing had happened."

"What happened to Foster? Was he still there?" Elizabeth asked.

"No, I don't know where he had disappeared to. But he was back later that evening. And before the night was over, Emily Marie was the happiest woman alive."

The Journals

The girls leaned forward, drinking in every word the elderly woman spoke. It seemed more like the makings of a romance movie than a real story.

The woman paused, and looked directly at Megan. "At closing time, Foster showed up again, wanting to talk to Emily Marie. They sat in one of the booths while I cleaned up. I tried to give them privacy and turned on the jukebox to a slow country song. But even over the music, I could hear bits and pieces of the conversation.

" 'Emily Marie, you must know how I feel about you. You must see it my eyes,' he told her. The whole thing was quite romantic. 'I want to spend the rest of my life with you. I'm going to sell my ranch in Colorado, and move down here, and we can get married. That is, if you'll have me,' he said.

"There she was, tears streaming down her cheeks. 'But Foster, I have my two kids to think about,' she said.

" 'I know I haven't met Ruby and Jack yet, but I promise I'll love them like my very own. I know things have been hard on you since your husband died. Let me rescue you,' he begged.

"Well, at that point I left the room. I figured the cleanup could wait. Emily Marie and I were best friends, and I had watched her struggle to make ends meet since Paul died. It looked to be a fairy-tale ending for her," Mrs. Wilson said as she leaned back in her chair.

The room was silent, except for the tick-ticking of the old grandfather clock in the corner. Finally, Megan broke the silence. "It sounds like my mom and my grandma had a lot in common. . . ."

Elizabeth reached over and squeezed her friend's hand.

"So what happened next?" Elizabeth asked.

Mrs. Wilson frowned. "The next few days are hard to talk about. I prefer to remember my friend in that moment, her face shining with joy."

The three girls remained silent. They didn't want to push the woman or be disrespectful, but they needed more information.

Jean Louise rescued them. "Mama, Megan wants to find out what happened to the marbles. Is there any more you can tell her?"

The woman looked at Megan again and smiled, a sad kind of smile. Then, she pulled herself up with her walker and started toward her bedroom. Jean Louise helped her mother, leaving the three girls alone in the living room.

"Why did she leave like that?" McKenzie whispered.

"I don't know, but it looks like she's our only hope for more information. We've got to find out what happened next," whispered Elizabeth.

Megan remained quiet, and Elizabeth put her arm around her friend. "This is hard for you, isn't it?" she asked.

"Not really. I mean, I never knew my grandmother. It's just strange that she and my mother were both young widows."

The girls heard the walker approaching and ended their whispered conversation. Jean Louise followed her mother, carrying several old notebooks. She handed them to Megan.

Mrs. Wilson was seated once again and took a moment to get settled. "These are my journals from that time. The whole story should be there, from the time Foster began coming to the restaurant, until. . ."

Megan looked at the books. It seemed she had just been handed her own treasure.

"You take them home and read them," the woman told her. "I hope they'll help you find what you're looking for."

Megan placed the journals on the coffee table in front of her, then walked to Mrs. Wilson's chair. She leaned over and hugged the woman. "Thank you so much," she said.

The old woman patted her on the shoulder, then wiped a tear from her wrinkled cheek. "You're welcome, my dear. You are more than welcome."

•—•—•

Back at the Big Texan, Megan had to report for work. "Here," she told Elizabeth, handing her the journals. "We can't afford to waste any time. Y'all start reading through these and see what you can find."

Elizabeth and McKenzie spent the better part of the morning by the Texas-shaped pool, reading through the yellowed pages and looking for clues. Much of what they found was insignificant—Mrs. Wilson's thoughts about her husband, her children, her job, even the price of groceries. Finally, McKenzie sat up in her lounge chair and said, "I found it! Listen to this: 'A man has been visiting the restaurant regularly and is obviously smitten with Emily Marie. He seems like a kind man. I hope she gives him a chance; she's been so sad since Paul died.' "

Elizabeth read over her friend's shoulder. "Jackpot!" she cried. "Now we have our starting point. Let's keep reading."

McKenzie wiped the sweat from her brow. "Okay," she said, "but can we continue this in the restaurant? I'm burning up out here, and I'm starving!"

"Me, too," agreed Elizabeth.

They gathered the journals and headed toward the restaurant. Passing the stables, they noticed a regal looking horse across the paddock. "Wow, what a beauty," said McKenzie. "Let's get a closer look."

They were about halfway there when they heard a man's

voice. It was Mr. Jacobs, leaning against the stable and talking on his cell phone. The girls shrank into the shadows of one of the stalls and remained silent.

"Yes, that's right," he said. "There were twelve marbles in a variety of gemstones. I tracked them to Amarillo, but it's been thirty years since anyone has seen or heard of them. They just vanished."

Jacobs began pacing in agitation. "I don't know how a set of priceless gemstone marbles can simply disappear. Surely somebody has to know something about them."

The man paused again, and then said, "I've got to find those marbles. I'm tired of all this rodeo business, never spending more than a week in the same place. I'm ready to settle down and live the good life, and those marbles will help me do it."

More silence, and then he said, "Okay. Let me know what you find out. I'll keep asking questions here." The man shut his cell phone and strode out of the stables and toward the hotel rooms.

"Whoa," said McKenzie. "That proves he's a crook."

"Not necessarily. But it does sound suspicious," said Elizabeth. "One thing is for sure. We're running out of time. We've got to locate those marbles before he does."

•—•—•

The girls kept their noses buried in the journals for the rest of the afternoon. The entries about Emily Marie were sporadic, interspersed with entries about housework and life as a waitress. It was like a treasure hunt—wading through the boring stuff to find the jewels.

Elizabeth liked the way Mrs. Wilson ended each journal entry with a one-sentence prayer. She felt she knew the old woman's heart better from those sentence prayers than from the actual journal entries.

Finally, after hours of searching, she found the following entry:

It seems that Foster, humble as he is, is very wealthy.

Tonight he gave Emily Marie a bag of marbles. But these aren't just any marbles, they're priceless gemstones!

The paperwork is even there—they're in her name.

She wasn't sure if she should keep such a gift, and fretted all evening. But after the restaurant closed, he showed up again and asked her to marry him!

Of course she accepted. But they won't make their plans known until he gets to know her children. He is a wonderful man, and I know he will be a good father to Ruby and Jack.

He's leaving town tonight. He told her to keep the marbles in a safe place, and he'll help her set up a safe-deposit box for them when he returns. She'll worry herself to death, carrying around something so priceless.

We talked about hiding them in the restaurant, but for tonight, she took them home. I'll bet she looks at them all night long.

Dear Father, please bless Emily Marie and her children with Your goodness. Amen.

"That's it! They're hidden in the restaurant!" shouted McKenzie.

Elizabeth shut the book and stood to stretch. Her eyes were tired from reading. "Maybe. Just like Alex suggested. But she could have gone ahead and put them in the bank, too. Why don't we head over and tell Megan what we've found. Maybe she can start snooping around."

"Yeah, and maybe we can get some more of that pie!" McKenzie added.

•—•—•

Later that night, the group sat in the stands at the Greater Amarillo Livestock Show and Rodeo. Mr. Jacobs had generously given them his entire section of box seats. "I'd love to have someone cheering for me," he'd said with a smile. His eyes had rested on Megan's mom.

James and Evan sat two rows in front of the girls, exclaiming over the horses, and making their own plans to be cowboys someday. Elizabeth was glad that, for now, her brother had a distraction.

Ruby Smith sat with the ladies making small talk, and the two dads seemed absorbed in a conversation about the Old Testament book of Isaiah. The three girls, satisfied they wouldn't be overheard, huddled together.

"So, did you find anything?" whispered McKenzie.

"No," answered Megan. "I need more information. I have no idea where to begin. I did examine the floor boards in the kitchen area, but I couldn't find any loose ones. I'm just not good at this detective business like the two of you are."

Elizabeth patted her friend on the knee. "You'll be fine. We just need to find more clues. We're not even sure they're at the restaurant. She might have put them in the bank or something. Do you think you can ask your mom if your grandma left any accounts open?"

"I've never heard her talk about any accounts. It seems that anything like that would have been closed out long ago. But I'll ask Mom tonight," Megan said.

"Ask Mom what?" Ruby Smith asked. The girls were surprised to find that she'd moved down and was now sitting directly behind them. Her hair was fixed in a new way, and she was wearing makeup.

"You look pretty tonight, Mom," Megan said. Mrs. Smith smiled.

"What did you want to ask me?" the woman persisted.

Megan smiled sheepishly. "You remember those jewels I talked to you about? We're still trying to find them."

Surprisingly, Mrs. Smith laughed. "Well, I'm afraid you're going on a wild-goose chase. But go ahead, ask me anything."

"Did Grandma leave any bank accounts open?" Megan asked. "We're wondering if she might not have stored the marbles in an account somewhere."

"Oh, you mean like in a safe-deposit box?" Mrs. Smith responded.

Elizabeth jumped in. "Exactly! Did your mother leave behind any kind of safe-deposit box?"

Mrs. Smith shook her head. "Not that I know of. But come to think of it, my grandmother did mention a small checking account. She never touched it. She said she wanted to leave it for me and Jack someday. It's still there."

"Bingo!" McKenzie shouted with excitement. "We've found the—"

Elizabeth clapped a hand over her friend's mouth. "Let's not announce it to the whole world," she said.

"Oh, yeah, sorry!" McKenzie whispered. "I tend to get a little excited."

The others chuckled good-naturedly. "It's okay," said Megan. "It is pretty exciting."

Mrs. Smith continued, "I have some business at the bank tomorrow anyway. I'll ask about the checking account. And since this is official mystery business, would you girls like to come with me? I'll take you all for ice cream afterwards."

The girls nodded, and Mrs. Smith returned to sit with the ladies.

Megan looked a little stunned, and Elizabeth asked, "What's wrong?"

"Who was that woman?" she asked.

Elizabeth turned and looked at Megan's mom, not sure how to respond to the question.

"My mom is fixing her hair, wearing makeup, coming to the rodeo. . .she's *smiling!* What has gotten into her?"

Elizabeth's and McKenzie's eyes swung to the handsome cowboy, sitting tall on a horse and getting ready to enter the arena.

No one answered Megan's question, but the looks of concern stayed on their faces for the rest of the evening.

•—•—•

The next morning, Elizabeth and McKenzie stared gloomily out the window of the Phillips' motel room. Rain poured down outside.

"I guess we won't do much sightseeing today," said McKenzie.

Elizabeth leaned over and lifted the stack of journals from the bedside table. "Well, as long as we're stuck here, we might as well read some more. Megan has to be at work at ten a.m., but she was going to come early and do some more snooping," she said, looking at her watch.

"Not snooping—*investigating,*" McKenzie corrected her friend.

Elizabeth chuckled. "Same thing," she said. "But *investigating* does sound more official, doesn't it?"

The girls settled in, sharing the same journal page, skimming for more clues. Before long, they found what they were looking for.

> *Emily Marie might go ahead and put the jewels in a safe-deposit box. She thought about doing it today, but it was late when she got off work, and the banks were already closed. Carrying around something so valuable is making her as nervous as a cat in a room full of rockers.*
>
> *She's anxious to put them in a safe place.*
>
> *She was headed to work a party at the Cadillac Ranch this evening. She said the pay is good and the tips are even better. She tried to get me to go with her, but I was just too tired tonight. I told her I'd go with her next time.*

McKenzie shut the book and hopped from the bed. "There you have it. She deposited the jewels. What time is Megan's mom taking us to the bank today?"

"I think at three thirty, when Megan gets off work. Why don't we walk to the restaurant and see if she's there yet?"

The two sleuths quickly headed toward the Big Texan Steak Ranch, staying close to the buildings to keep from getting wet. They rushed through the swinging saloon-style doors, straight into a plaid cowboy shirt. Leaning their necks back, they looked up, up, up to see the owner of the shirt. It was Mr. Jacobs.

"Good mornin', ladies," he said, and tipped his big white cowboy hat. True to form, he winked at them before he strode out the door.

The girls didn't know whether to be angry or giggle. "I wish he didn't look so much like a movie star," McKenzie said.

"Why?" Elizabeth asked.

"Because it would be a lot easier not to like him," she replied seriously.

Just then, Jean Louise appeared. "What is it with you early birds this morning?" she asked. "Megan's already been here for twenty minutes, cleaning every nook and cranny of the supply room. She's not even clocked in yet."

The two girls looked at each other and then at the red-haired waitress. "Uhm, could we, uh. . ." Elizabeth stammered.

"Go on back," she said, pointing the way. "But if the manager catches you, she may put you to work."

The girls dashed through the kitchen area to the dark

storage room. They pushed open the door, and Megan gasped.

"You scared me!" she whispered, looking guilty. "Quick, close the door!"

The Costumes

The girls entered the small room and shut the door behind them. Megan was on her knees, surrounded by cans of tomato paste. She held a dust rag in her hand and appeared to be cleaning the bottom shelf.

"Look at this," she said.

The girls leaned forward, but the dim lighting made it difficult to see. "Isn't there a better light in here?" Elizabeth asked.

"One of the bulbs is burned out," Megan told her. "But you can still see if you look close enough."

McKenzie got down on her knees and examined the wall where Megan was cleaning. Elizabeth bent low and looked over her shoulder. Sure enough, there was a square break in the paneling, just large enough for a small teenage girl to crawl through.

"Do you think it's a secret passageway?" McKenzie asked.

"I don't know what it is. I haven't been able to get it open. There are a couple of screws, but I need a screwdriver. Do you think the marbles could be hidden here?"

"That's what we were coming to talk to you about," Elizabeth told Megan. "We read in the journal that Emily Marie was planning to put the marbles in a safe-deposit box at the bank. We may be wasting our time here."

Megan looked at Elizabeth, then McKenzie, her mouth hanging open. "You mean I've been breaking my back in here for nothing?" she said.

McKenzie chuckled. "Well, look on the bright side. Just think how impressed your boss will be that you spent your free time cleaning out the supply room."

The three girls returned the cans to the lower shelf and left the small room.

"It's time for me to clock in," said Megan, looking at her watch. "I'll see you both this afternoon. Maybe we'll actually find the marbles!"

Elizabeth and McKenzie left the kitchen and spotted the Phillips family at a corner table in the restaurant. "Come on," McKenzie said. "Let's join them. I'm starved!"

"Me, too," agreed Elizabeth.

Before long they were each devouring a tall stack of pancakes, drenched in syrup and covered with whipped cream. Outside the window, the sun peeked through the clouds. The rain had stopped.

As they ate, Mr. and Mrs. Phillips asked, "So, what do you want to do today?"

The girls both shrugged their shoulders and kept eating.

They were having fun, as long as they were together.

"I'd like to go shopping," said Mrs. Phillips. "I saw some little boutiques a few blocks over."

Evan groaned, and Mr. Phillips shifted in his seat. "Why don't you girls go shopping, and Evan and I will hang out here with the horses and the cowboys?" the man suggested.

The girls nodded, and before long, the three females headed toward Amarillo's shopping district.

•—•—•

In and out of shops they went, looking at Texas-shaped handbags encrusted with rhinestones, flashy cowgirl boots and hats, and western wear in all colors and sizes. Before they knew it, two hours had passed.

They were on their way back to the motel when McKenzie spotted a fun-looking thrift shop. "Oh, I want to see what they have in there, Mom," she said.

"I want to run across the street to the post office and get some stamps," Mrs. Phillips said, waving a handful of postcards. "Why don't you two go over there, and I'll meet you after I mail these."

The girls entered the old store and were thrilled at the endless racks of vintage clothing, hats, and scarves. McKenzie wasted no time trying on a dark pair of sunglasses, an oversize hat, and a feather boa.

Elizabeth laughed at her friend's outfit and then spotted a large cardboard box filled with wigs. Within moments, she was a brunette with long, messy curls.

The girls giggled as they tried an array of wigs, scarves, and jewelry. They were completely unrecognizable when the bell over the door jangled. The two looked toward the entrance expecting to find Mrs. Phillips. Instead, Mark Jacobs walked toward them, a serious look on his face.

They froze. What in the world could a cowboy like Mr. Jacobs want in a girlie thrift shop like this? The man nodded at the girls, but kept walking. He didn't recognize them!

He approached the counter and asked to speak to the shop's owner. The clerk went to the back of the store and returned with an elegant, gray-haired woman.

"How may I help you?" she asked.

The cowboy introduced himself, then asked, "How long have you owned this shop?"

"Oh, I inherited this business from my grandparents. This little shop has been in our family since it opened, over forty years ago," she told him.

"I'm trying to track down a rare set of marbles," he said. "The last record I can find of them is here in Amarillo, about thirty years ago. I heard they were given to a poor waitress. I'm wondering if she sold them."

Elizabeth and McKenzie moved a little closer to the counter. They pretended to be looking at some jewelry, and the two adults paid no attention to them.

"Marbles? I don't recall any unusual marbles. Every now

and then we've bought little toys like that, but we sell them pretty quickly. Usually to a young mother who is in here shopping," she told him.

"Oh, these marbles weren't toys. I'm sure the woman wouldn't have sold them cheaply. They were very valuable," he told her.

The woman thought a moment, wrinkling her brow in concentration. "No, I'm sorry. I don't recall anything like that."

Mr. Jacobs looked disappointed. He tipped his hat to the woman, thanked her, and headed out the door.

The girls stared after him, mouths hanging open, when the clerk startled them. "Can I help you find something?"

Elizabeth and McKenzie began taking off their costumes and returning them to the proper places. "Oh, no thank you. We were just having a little fun. This is a great shop you have," Elizabeth told her.

The bell jangled again as Mrs. Phillips walked through the door.

"Are you ready, girls?" she asked.

"Yes, ma'am," they called, and left the store. They wanted to discuss the scene they'd just witnessed, but that conversation would have to wait.

Back at the motel, Elizabeth and McKenzie exchanged frustrated looks. They hadn't found a moment of privacy since they were at the shop. First they had stopped at Dairy

Queen for hamburgers. Then Mrs. Phillips had asked the girls to entertain Evan for a while.

They were about to meet Megan when the phone rang. "It's for you, Elizabeth," said Mr. Phillips. It was her mom.

"Hi, baby. Are you having fun?" Mrs. Anderson asked.

"Yes, ma'am. We've been busy today."

"That's good. Listen, I know Ruby is taking you to the bank, and then for ice cream. After that, why don't you swing back by the hotel and pick up Evan? I've already talked to the Phillipses about this. You all can spend the evening over here so McKenzie's parents can have a date."

Elizabeth groaned inwardly, but said only, "Yes, ma'am." Evan was a nice kid, but two little boys could put a real wrench in their sleuthing plans. After hanging up, she shared the news with McKenzie, who did groan. Loudly.

Mr. and Mrs. Phillips looked at the girls and chuckled.

With a wave, the two girls finally escaped to the restaurant. When the door shut behind them, they began their frantic whispers.

"Can you believe that man? Calling Megan's grandmother a 'poor waitress,' like she was some charity case. And who does he think he is, anyway? It's none of his business!" McKenzie said.

"Well, technically, she was a poor waitress. But we know the rest of the story, and he doesn't. I wonder how he knows that much, though," Elizabeth responded. The sun had disappeared behind some more gray clouds, and the storm threatened to return.

Rounding the corner, they found Megan and her mom waiting for them. Mrs. Smith was dressed in her maid's uniform. Her hair was coming out of its clip, and she wore no makeup. Still, Elizabeth thought she looked more like a runway model than a maid.

"Hop in, everyone. The quicker we get to the bank, the quicker we can hit The Marble Slab," said the woman, referring to the popular ice cream shop.

All three girls climbed into the backseat of the old sedan, and Ruby Smith laughed. "I feel like a chauffeur," she told them.

On the way to the bank, McKenzie and Elizabeth whispered to Megan, telling her about the event in the thrift shop.

They were interrupted by Mrs. Smith. "Am I supposed to be hearing this?" she asked. "Because I can hear almost every word you are saying. Something about a tall cowboy in a girlie thrift store? That must have been a funny sight."

The girls laughed nervously but stopped talking. They didn't want Mrs. Smith to know about Mr. Jacobs. Not yet, anyway.

They pulled into the bank parking lot, slid out of the car, and went inside the old building. "You all wait here while I make my deposits," Mrs. Smith told them, gesturing to a long bench. "After that, I have an appointment with Mr. Sanders, the bank's vice president. Megan, you can come with me and tell him what you've heard."

The girls took a seat and waited as Mrs. Smith approached the teller. A few minutes later, she joined the girls on the bench.

Before long, a balding man approached. "Hello, Ruby," he said. "This is a lovely group you have with you."

Ruby smiled and introduced the girls, and then she and Megan entered the office to the left of the bench. The door was pushed shut, but it bounced open just a crack.

Elizabeth and McKenzie scooted closer to the door, hoping to hear the conversation. They heard bits and pieces and knew Megan would fill them in on the details later. Still, they strained to catch the words being spoken.

Mrs. Smith's voice was soft and sweet. They heard, ". . .my mother. . .bank account. . .curious. . ."

Then the banker's voice, "Yes. . .did leave. . .lovely woman. . .still open. . . interest. . ."

They heard Mrs. Smith's voice again, "Megan. . . rumors. . .safe-deposit box. . ."

Megan added something to the conversation, but the girls couldn't make out the words. Didn't she know to speak up when her friends were eavesdropping?

There was a shuffling of some papers, then a faint noise. Was he typing on a computer?

The banker's voice came back. "No. . .record. . .safe deposit. . .nothing. . ."

There was a scooting of chairs, and the two girls on the bench slid to their original positions. The door opened, and Mr. Sanders shook Mrs. Smith's hand. "I'm sorry I couldn't help you more," he said. "Good day, ladies."

Megan looked disappointed, and Mrs. Smith patted her on the back. "It would have been nice to have found those mysterious marbles. But we've done fine without them, haven't we? We don't need a hidden treasure. I have all the treasure I need in you, sweet girl."

Megan smiled at her mother and gave her a hug. But Elizabeth knew this wasn't the end of the search. The group headed out the door. The mystery would have to wait; it was time for ice cream.

•—•—•

Back at Elizabeth's house, the girls shut the door to her bedroom. The young detectives were ready to talk seriously.

"Tell me again what happened at the thrift shop," Megan said.

Elizabeth and McKenzie took turns telling the story, and Megan laughed out loud when she heard about the costumes. "I wish I had been there!" she said. "I can just see you two, all decked out in sunglasses and wigs. You must have looked ridiculous!"

"Actually, we looked pretty good," said Elizabeth.

McKenzie giggled. "Uhm, Elizabeth, I hate to tell you this, but that black wig did not look good on you! You definitely can't pull it off like Hannah Montana can. I think you need to stay a blond," she said.

Elizabeth laughed. "Come to think of it, your freckles did look rather out of place with that yellow wig. And those tiny little sunglasses!"

"Well you looked like a demented movie star with those huge things you were wearing!"

All three girls were on the floor now, laughing at the silliness of it all.

Before they could get any further in the story, they heard a thud on Elizabeth's door. Then another, and another. Elizabeth got up and opened her door, only to have a miniature car crash into her ankle. "Ouch!" she cried.

James and Evan sat on the floor at the end of the hallway, with Matchbox cars lined up in front of them. "Sorry, Beth. We're racing," said James.

Elizabeth sighed a heavy sigh. "Why can't you do that in your bedroom?" she asked her brother.

"Because there's not enough space," he told her matter-of-factly. She stepped to his doorway and saw what he meant. Toys were scattered across every inch of the floor.

"You'd better clean up that mess before Mom sees," she told him.

James looked crestfallen. "But that will take too long,"

he said. "I want to race with Evan."

Elizabeth felt a wave of compassion for her little brother. He really was a good kid, even if he was annoying at times. "I'll tell you what. You and Evan pick up your toys, and then we'll sit with you in the driveway so you can race out there."

James looked at his sister as if she were his hero. He wasn't allowed in the front yard without supervision, but he loved to race his cars up and down the long driveway.

Just then, a loud clap of thunder startled them all. James's face fell, and he said, "We can't. It's raining."

Sure enough, it looked like the heavens had opened up. Lightning flashed, rain poured in heavy sheets, and water gushed off the sidewalks and into the gutters.

Another loud crash of thunder was followed by a pop, and everything went black.

The girls squealed and huddled together.

James and Evan stayed seated at the end of the hallway. Through the dark, they heard Evan's voice saying, "This is so cool!"

Then James said, "Hey, let's race cars in the dark!"

A moment later, Elizabeth yelped in pain. Another flash of lightning revealed that a Hot Wheels car had crashed into her ankle. Again. "James, cut that out!"

"Sorry, Beth," he said. She shut her door, leaving the boys in the black hallway.

The three girls gathered at the window to watch the show. Thunder clapped. A fierce wind forced the trees to sway into unnatural positions. Somewhere in the distance a car alarm went off. The whole scene was scary and fascinating.

Suddenly, a pair of headlights pulled into Megan's driveway, behind her mom's car. They shut off, and all was black again.

"I wonder who that could be," Megan said.

They peered through the darkness, trying to catch a glimpse of the unknown guest. A flash of lightning revealed a tall dark figure in a cowboy hat, heading for Megan's porch.

Through the Hole in the Wall

The three girls gasped. They peered through the darkness, hoping to catch another glimpse of the man.

"What in the world is he doing here?" asked McKenzie.

"I don't know, but my mom is alone. We've got to do something!" said Megan.

"I'll grab my flashlight. Megan, you unlock my window. We'll crawl through and stay hidden until we can figure out what's going on." Elizabeth felt around in the dark, pulling open the drawer to her bedside table. Locating the flashlight, she clicked it on and returned to the window, which was now wide open. Wind and rain gushed through, getting her curtains all wet.

The three girls slipped through the window, and Elizabeth pulled it shut behind her. She would have a lot of explaining to do if her parents found the wet room, but this was important. Ruby was in danger.

The girls ran, staying low to the ground. *Pow!* Rain soaked their skin. *Crash!* A flash of lightning revealed an empty porch. Mr. Jacobs's truck was still parked in the driveway.

"Come on!" Megan called out. Through the window, Ruby appeared to be lighting candles. Soon their soft glow gave light for the girls to see what was going on.

Jacobs spoke, but they couldn't hear the words. Ruby laughed. Then Mr. Jacobs began moving around the house with the flashlight!

"He's looking for the marbles," McKenzie said.

"But why is she letting him?" asked Elizabeth. "That doesn't make sense."

"Somebody has to stop him," said Megan. She stood and pushed open her front door.

Ruby Smith was startled. "Megan? What are you doing out in this weather? I thought you were at Elizabeth's house!"

Elizabeth and McKenzie appeared in the doorway. The girls shivered like puppies fresh from a bath, dripping water all over the hardwood floor.

"Oh my goodness! Girls, get in here. Let me find you some towels." Ruby pulled the girls inside and shut the door behind them.

Mr. Jacobs appeared from the hallway. "What on earth? Girls, are you okay?"

Ruby picked up a candle and brushed past Mr. Jacobs into the hallway. She returned with an armload of thick, fluffy towels. Each girl took one and dried herself. Suddenly, there was a loud *Pop!* and the electricity returned.

The house lit up, and the television began broadcasting

the Home and Garden network, Ruby's favorite. Weather updates scrolled across the bottom of the screen.

Ruby stood, hands on hips, looking at the girls. Finally, her eyes rested on Megan. "Explain yourself, young lady. Why would you go running around in a storm like this? You could have gotten struck by lightning!"

Elizabeth and McKenzie looked at their sopping shoes. Megan lifted her chin and said, "We were worried about you, Mama. We were in Elizabeth's room, and we saw a strange car pull into the driveway, and. . ." her eyes flashed to Mr. Jacobs. "And we saw a man coming onto our porch."

Mr. Jacobs stepped forward. "Well, now, that would be scary. That was very brave of you to come and check on your mother. I'm sorry. I never meant to frighten anyone."

Megan held the man's eyes, as if waiting for an explanation. She was usually very respectful to her elders. But she was also very protective of her mother.

Jacobs continued. "I was driving a couple of blocks from here when the power went out. I thought of you and your mama here by yourselves. I thought I'd come check on you." The man shifted his cowboy hat from one hand to the other, then back again. He looked nervous.

Megan held his eyes but said nothing. Elizabeth and McKenzie watched the scene. The electric clock on the side table flashed on and off, on and off.

Mr. Jacobs said, "Well, it looks like everyone is okay, so

I guess I'll head back to the motel. Sorry to have frightened you girls."

Ruby held out her arm in protest. "Oh, don't go before I can fix you a cup of coffee. You're soaking wet! Here, take a towel."

The man smiled gently at Ruby and said, "Aww, no ma'am. I'll be fine. But thank you." With that, he tipped his hat to her and left.

Ruby Smith's eyes swung to the girls standing in front of her, landing on her daughter. "Let's get you three warmed up. Then, you have some tall talkin' to do."

The girls followed the woman into the kitchen and sat around the oak table as Mrs. Smith made hot cocoa. While the water was boiling, she picked up the phone and dialed. "Sue? This is Ruby. The girls are at my house. I just wanted you to know they're safe. . . . No, they haven't explained themselves yet. We're getting to that. . . . Okay, I'll see one of you in a minute."

Elizabeth groaned inwardly. How would she explain sneaking out the window? It hadn't seemed like a bad idea at the time. But now, it was going to be hard to defend.

Moments later, there was a knock at the door, and Ruby rushed to let Robert Anderson in. He didn't look happy. "Elizabeth, what were you thinking? The boys said you sneaked out your window! And in a storm? That's not like you at all. Explain, young lady."

Elizabeth took a deep breath and sent a desperate plea to heaven. "We weren't trying to be bad. We just got scared, and the electricity was off, and then we saw Mr. Jacobs coming toward the porch, and we knew Megan's mom was here by herself, and—"

"Wait a minute," interrupted Ruby. "You knew it was Mr. Jacobs? It sounded to me like you thought he was a stranger!"

Megan answered. "Mom, we thought it might be Mr. Jacobs, but we didn't know for sure. And there's more. We don't trust him."

The two adults looked at each other and then at the girls. Elizabeth's dad sat down and leaned forward. "We've got all night. Start talking."

The girls remained silent, not knowing where to begin. Finally, Elizabeth and Megan began pouring out the story from beginning to end, one pausing as the other jumped in, back and forth like a tennis match. McKenzie added a detail here and there.

The two adults looked at the girls, stunned. "So you've been trying to solve a mystery?" asked Mr. Anderson.

The girls nodded. Elizabeth's dad leaned back in his chair, and a great belly laugh erupted that continued for several minutes. The girls weren't sure how to respond.

Mrs. Smith chuckled, too, but she appeared to be laughing more at her neighbor than at the situation.

Finally, the man pulled himself together and gave Elizabeth a stern look. "I'm glad you wanted to help Megan's mom. But what you did was foolish. First of all, it is never okay to sneak out your window, unless something dangerous is inside the house, like a fire. Second, it is never okay to go running around in a storm. You all could have been seriously hurt. Third, it was foolish of you to think you could save Mrs. Smith from any man. You should have come to me immediately."

Elizabeth looked at her father. She hated disappointing him. "I'm sorry, Daddy."

"You're forgiven," he said. "But you still have to be punished. I'm not going to ground you while McKenzie is here. But when the Phillips's vacation is over, you're going to be seeing a lot of the inside of our house."

•—•—•

Later that night, McKenzie and Elizabeth lay awake whispering. Their room at the Big Texan had a small living area with a pullout bed, which gave the girls some privacy.

"Did you notice that my dad and Megan's mom weren't concerned about Mr. Jacobs?" Elizabeth asked.

"Yeah, I did," whispered McKenzie. "Your dad thought the whole thing was funny."

"My dad has a good sense about people. But the fact that Mr. Jacobs is looking for the marbles is strange," she said. "Maybe we should just come out and ask him about it."

McKenzie thought. "No. He clearly has plans for those marbles. But Megan and her mom could use the money. I'm still not sure I trust him."

"Me neither," replied Elizabeth. "We have to find those marbles before he does."

The girls were quiet for a few minutes. Then McKenzie rolled to face her friend. "Hey, Elizabeth. . .since the marbles never made it to the bank, I wonder if they really are hidden at the restaurant."

"I was thinking that, too. We'll go there first thing in the morning," she said sleepily.

•—•—•

The two sleuths were awake and dressed before dawn the next morning. They walked to the restaurant, which was open early for breakfast. A waitress they'd not seen before seated them, and the girls studied the menu.

"We need to get into that supply closet," said Elizabeth, her eyes scanning the walls and floor planks. "That secret panel seems like the perfect hiding place."

"What time does Megan come in?" asked McKenzie.

Elizabeth's eyes focused on someone behind McKenzie, and a grin spread across her face. "Right now," she said.

McKenzie turned to find Megan walking toward them. "I see we all had the same idea," she said. "I think we need to check that supply closet again."

Elizabeth scooted over in the booth to make room

for her friend. "Did you and your mom talk any more last night?" she asked.

"Yeah. I ended up sleeping in her bed and we talked for a long time. She does think it's weird that Mr. Jacobs is looking for the marbles. She promised to keep her distance from him," Megan told them.

The other two girls observed something in Megan's attitude that seemed. . .not quite right. "You don't seem happy," said McKenzie.

Megan let out a heavy sigh. "It's just that my mom's been through so much. I wasn't thrilled when Mr. Jacobs flirted with her. But he made her smile! She was singing, and humming. For the last few days, she's seemed happier. I just hate that he's a fake."

Elizabeth thought about that. "He might not be a fake. My dad doesn't have a problem with him, and you know my dad. He's pretty good about figuring people out," she said.

"Maybe so, Elizabeth, but he's definitely after those marbles. We can't let him find them before we do," McKenzie said.

"I have a feeling that when we find the marbles, we'll find out the answers to a lot of our questions about Mr. Jacobs," McKenzie told them.

After a moment, Megan stood and said, "Well, we won't find them sitting in this booth. Let's get started. Come with me."

The girls followed their friend through the restaurant, into the kitchen area, and to the supply room. The early morning manager, a friendly-looking woman in her early fifties, said, "You're here early, Megan!"

"Uh, yes, Mrs. Edgar. I really want to get that supply closet cleaned out. My friends have volunteered to help."

The woman gave them a strange look, but smiled. "Interesting. I suppose it's a better way to spend your time than sitting in front of the television. It's good to see young people with a sense of responsibility. Have fun!"

The girls entered the supply closet, and Megan flipped on the dim light. "I guess I'll have to fix that light myself," she said, grabbing a stepladder. "McKenzie, could you hand me one of those bulbs behind you?"

McKenzie did as she was asked. Elizabeth got on her hands and knees. She moved the tomato cans away from the hidden panel.

"Megan, do you know where a Phillips screwdriver is?" she asked.

"Well, I know where a Phillips is," Megan responded, and she and McKenzie laughed. It took a moment for Elizabeth to catch on to the joke about McKenzie's last name, but when she did, she laughed, too. After a few minutes, the light-bulb was changed. Elizabeth was on her stomach unscrewing the panel in the wall. When the last screw was loose, the panel was removed to reveal a small square.

Elizabeth reached inside and felt around but found nothing. "This hole goes pretty far back. One of us will have to go in with a flashlight."

The three girls stood looking at each other, trying to decide who was least likely to get stuck. All three were slim but had different shapes and builds. Finally, McKenzie and Megan said in unison, "Elizabeth is the skinniest."

"Hey!" Elizabeth said, then looked down at her long arms and legs. "Okay, I guess I'm skinny. But so are y'all."

"Slim, yes. String beans? No. You're the only string bean in the bunch," said Megan.

Elizabeth sighed good-naturedly. "I knew I should have gotten three scoops of ice cream yesterday. . . ," she muttered. "Where is Kate when we need her?"

McKenzie laughed at the memory of their tiny camp friend. Kate had made them all look like giants.

Megan got a flashlight from the office, and Elizabeth shimmied into the opening. The beam from the light revealed years of accumulated dust, a crack in the concrete floor, and a few dead bugs. There was even an old label from a green bean can, which looked as if it had been there for decades. "Cool!" Elizabeth called out, examining the label.

"What did you find?" asked Megan.

"This old green bean label must be older than our parents!" she called.

Megan and McKenzie shared exasperated looks. "The

marbles, Elizabeth! Stay focused," Megan called out.

Mrs. Edgar pushed the door open and poked her head in. "Megan, dear, since you're here early, why don't you clock in? We're shorthanded this morning. I may let you try waitressing."

Megan and McKenzie jumped and turned to block the pair of legs that were sticking out of the wall.

"Yes, ma'am," Megan said.

"Pronto," the woman said, shooing the two girls out of the supply room. "I thought there were three of you," she questioned.

Suddenly, a loud crash came from the kitchen, followed by a yelp. "Jessie, how many times do I have to tell you to wear oven mitts?" Mrs. Edgar said to a young man across the room. She closed the door, leaving Megan and McKenzie wondering what to do next. The woman called over her shoulder, "Megan, show your friend out of the kitchen. Too many people are back here as it is. Then go sign in and report to the waitress's station."

Trapped!

Elizabeth heard the muffled voices. She tried to draw her feet up into the hole, but something caught on her blue jeans. She was trapped! She couldn't wiggle backward or forward.

The voices faded, and she heard a loud crash, followed by the click of a door. Somehow, she knew she'd been left alone. She tried to shine her flashlight to find what was catching her jeans, but she couldn't wiggle her body that way in the tight space. She finally gave up and decided to wait.

Lord, what have I gotten myself into? she prayed silently into the darkness. *What will my dad say? He'll tell me I should have known better than to go crawling around in holes in buildings. But Lord, we have to find those marbles! Please help us.*

Elizabeth made herself as comfortable as possible and waited. After a while, she shined her light on the green bean label. Not very interesting.

She heard a sound above her head like running water. Shining her light, she tilted her head backward to find pipes. Water pipes. *So that's the reason for the panel. To let the plumber work on the pipes.*

"I wish I had a book or something," she whispered. Then, it dawned on her. The journals! In their excitement to solve the mystery, she and McKenzie had abandoned Mrs. Wilson's journals. But what if there was more?

How could we have been so blind? Elizabeth mentally berated herself for jumping to conclusions and not reading the journals at least to the end of Emily Marie's story. Her mind raced with the possibilities of those journals when she heard another click. She felt two hands on her ankles.

"Hello?" she called in a soft voice. "Who's there?"

Through the darkness, she heard a familiar twang. "What have you gotten yourself into? Gracious sakes alive, girl! Here, your jeans are caught. Be still, now. Okay, I'm gonna pull."

After a few tugs from behind, Elizabeth was able to back herself out of the hole. She sat up, looked into Jean Louise's face, and sighed with relief. "Oh, Jean Louise! Am I glad to see you! I was scared I was going to—"

"You should be whipped, young lady! What kind of stunt do you think you're pulling? Why, there could be rats in those walls, or loose wires. . ."

Elizabeth shuddered. She hadn't considered those possibilities.

"And you could have been arrested for breaking and

entering. You have no business being back here!" the woman continued.

Elizabeth blinked back tears. "I—I'm sorry, Jean Louise. We were only—"

The woman grabbed her and hugged her. "Now don't you start crying. I'm just glad you're okay. You better be thankful I was on duty! When the girls told me what y'all were up to, I just about died. I've got to get back. Come on, now, dust yourself off. And no more crawling around in holes, ya' hear me?"

Elizabeth nodded and promised. Jean Louise pushed open the supply room door. When the coast was clear, the two headed out of the kitchen.

Out front, Megan was frantically taking orders. When she saw Elizabeth, she smiled, but continued her work. Mac was waiting on a bench near the entrance and stood when she saw her friend. Without a word, the two girls headed back to the motel room.

•—•—•

Several hours later, Elizabeth and McKenzie were stretched out by the Texas-shaped pool. Elizabeth read aloud from Mrs. Wilson's journal, while McKenzie listened. They were determined to read to the end of the story this time.

> *Dear God, I can't believe this is happening. Why Emily Marie? Why now? Lord, You knew her car*

was going to break down. You knew she would be out alone after dark. Why couldn't You have stopped this from happening?

Oh, I'm not blaming You, Lord. It just doesn't make any sense. She's got those two precious children, and now Foster. Why did that car have to hit her?

If only I had gone with her, like she asked. Maybe then, none of this would have happened. Oh, God, please let her be okay. It doesn't look good.

I sat with her tonight, Lord. She talked a lot, but she didn't make much sense. She kept asking about her babies, and then saying something about the big blue fin. She's hallucinating, Lord. I tried to hold her hand and comfort her. But she just kept telling me to look under the fin.

The next few pages told of Emily Marie's death and funeral. After that, the journal entries ended until nearly a year later, but nothing more was said about Emily Marie.

The girls thumbed back through the pages, trying to find something more that would help them. But it was no use. They found no more hidden clues.

McKenzie sat up in her lounge chair. "The big blue fin," she said. "What a strange thing to say."

Then, as if reading one another's mind, they both started talking at once. "The fish! Isn't there a—"

"A big fish! In the restaurant!"

"Yeah, it's hanging on that back wall! It's a—a swordfish or something!"

"A blue marlin, I think the sign said!"

The girls looked at each other, excitement flashing in their eyes, and started for the restaurant. They were halfway there when they realized they were wearing their swimsuits.

They practically ran back to their room and changed, and were at the restaurant in no time.

Jean Louise greeted them at the door. "Well, well. If it isn't Bonnie and Clyde."

Elizabeth laughed at the comment, then leaned over and whispered, "We think we may have found the marbles."

Jean Louise's eyes grew wide, and Elizabeth continued. "Can you seat us at that table under the big fish? Your mom put something in her journal about a blue fin."

The waitress looked skeptical, but led them through the restaurant. "That fish has been hanging there since I can remember. Just don't go crawling through any more holes in the wall without telling me first. I don't want to be bailing you kids out of jail."

The girls laughed and took their seats. They were thrilled to be sitting right beneath the fish, and felt certain this would be the end of their search.

They examined the fish closely. McKenzie lightly tapped the wall under the fish, but stopped when the people next to them looked curiously.

Elizabeth picked up the crisp linen napkin from the table. She dropped it on the floor. Crawling under the table to retrieve it, she examined the wall and floor. Suddenly, she felt a tap on her shoulder. Turning to find Jean Louise's white work shoes, Elizabeth scrambled out from under the table. She banged her head.

"Ouch!" she cried.

Jean Louise showed little sympathy. "Elizabeth Anderson, I don't know what I'm going to do with you."

"But Jean Lou—"

"Don't 'But Jean Louise' me! You'll get in big trouble if you don't stop poking around." The woman sighed and placed her hands on her hips. "I'll tell you what. The restaurant closes at ten p.m. If you can be here then, I'll let you look to your heart's content. I'll even help you. But you have to leave well enough alone while the customers are here."

Elizabeth jumped from her seat and hugged the woman. "Oh, thank you, Jean Louise! You're my hero! I just know we're going to find the—"

"Shhh! Not so loud. You never know who might be listening." She gestured toward the opposite corner of the restaurant, and they noticed Mr. Jacobs for the first time. He was looking at them strangely. When they made eye contact, he waved.

Elizabeth sat back in her seat. "Okay. We'll meet you here at closing time," she said. The woman left them, and McKenzie and Elizabeth leaned their heads together, trying to decide whether the marbles would end up being in the floor or the wall.

"Just think. We may be sitting on them right now," McKenzie said.

Elizabeth's eyes grew round. "They could be in the booth! What if she pulled the stuffing out of one of the benches and put them in there?"

"They've probably replaced the benches since then," McKenzie told her. Their eyes grew wide at the thought. They pushed it aside and decided to deal with that possibility when the time came.

•—•—•

Back at the motel room, Mr. and Mrs. Phillips were looking at travel brochures. "We only have a few days left in our vacation, and we want to make the most of them. There's a water park, a cowboy museum, and the famous Cadillac Ranch," said Mr. Phillips.

"There's also an outlet mall I'd like to visit, and a zoo," added Mrs. Phillips. "What are you all interested in?"

"Water park!" shouted McKenzie.

"Cadillac Ranch!" shouted Evan.

Elizabeth remained quiet.

Mrs. Phillips placed the brochures to the water park

and the Cadillac Ranch to one side. "That nice man, Mr. Jacobs, offered to take us back to the rodeo grounds and let us see the livestock up close. There's also a fair with the rodeo," she said while reading over some of the brochures. "We'll probably go there this afternoon."

"Cool!" said Evan. "Do you think he'll let me ride a bull?"

"No, but you might be able to ride a real rodeo horse," his father told him.

"Dad, are you going to buy that horse from him?" McKenzie asked.

"I'm thinking about it. He seems pretty anxious to sell. Says he wants to buy a house near here. But he's not sure what will happen until some inheritance of his comes through."

"Inheritance?" McKenzie and Elizabeth asked at once.

"Yeah, apparently his uncle left behind some priceless . . .marbles or something. But they've disappeared. Jacobs is trying to track them down."

Elizabeth stood and grabbed McKenzie by the arm. "I just remembered something I wanted to look at down at the gift shop," she said.

"Okay, girls. Stay close," said Mrs. Phillips.

As soon as the door closed behind them, McKenzie looked at Elizabeth questioningly.

"I have an idea. We've been skirting around Mr. Jacobs, trying to go behind his back. But since he's so interested in those marbles, why don't we go straight to him?"

McKenzie's eyes grew wide. "You mean just come out and ask him?"

"No. I have a plan," Elizabeth told her friend. They headed to the gift shop, where they purchased sidewalk chalk and a bag of marbles.

A half hour later, the two young detectives sat on the sidewalk near Mr. Jacobs's room, casually playing a game of marbles. Elizabeth had drawn a large circle using the sidewalk chalk, and the two girls took turns thumping their shooter marbles, trying to knock the other's marbles out of the circle. They were absorbed in the game and didn't notice when the door behind them quietly opened and shut.

McKenzie noticed the embroidered cowboy boots first. They were behind Elizabeth, who was concentrating on which angle to shoot her marbles. McKenzie's eyes followed the long legs up, up, up, until she looked into the amused eyes of Mr. Jacobs.

"You know, if you shoot to the left, it will ricochet and knock out the marbles on the right," he said.

Elizabeth nearly jumped out of her skin, even though she'd expected him. "Oh, hi, Mr. Jacobs!" she told him after she regained her composure. "Are we in your way? We're sorry."

"Oh, no, not at all," the man told her. "I love a good game of marbles." He eyed the colorful balls with interest.

The two shifted into sleuth mode. "Really? Are you a

marble expert?" McKenzie asked the man.

He stepped off the curb and sat on the sidewalk next to them. "I guess you could say that. I've played marbles since I was a little boy."

"Really? Not too many people play the game anymore. Did someone special teach you how?" Elizabeth asked.

"Yep," said the cowboy. "My uncle. He was more like a father to me than anything. He never married or had children, but he loved me like I was his son."

"Really?" Elizabeth probed him. Her plan was working perfectly. "Do you still see him a lot?"

"Unfortunately, no," he said. "He passed away about a year ago. But he had a soft spot in his heart for Amarillo. Never told me why, though. I suspect he fell in love here. He never talked much about the time he spent here. But whenever he mentioned Amarillo, he got a distant look in his eyes."

The girls remained quiet and let the man talk.

"I really miss him. I've decided to settle here, since he seemed to love the place so much."

"What was your uncle's name?" Elizabeth asked. Just then, Evan rounded the corner.

"McKenzie, Mama says to come. We're going to the fair," the boy told his sister.

Mr. Jacobs stood up and said, "I need to be going, too. Nice talking with you girls." And with that, he left.

The girls gathered up their marbles as Evan watched. "Those are cool," he said. "Where did you get them?"

Elizabeth replaced the colorful round balls into their drawstring pouch and handed them to Evan. "Here you go. I got them at the gift shop, but you can have them," she told him.

"Cool! Thanks, Elizabeth!" he said.

The three of them walked back to the Phillips's motel room, where McKenzie's parents were waiting. "Elizabeth, call your mom and ask if it's okay if we pick up James. He'd probably enjoy a day at the fair, don't you think?" Mrs. Phillips asked.

A short time later, the four Phillipses and the two younger Andersons were *oohing* and *ahhing* over the sights at the fair. Elizabeth and Evan held dripping ice cream cones, while McKenzie and James opted for cotton candy.

They rode the Ferris wheel and held their arms high during the roller coaster ride. While they walked along a row of games, James spotted the balloon darts. He wasn't looking at the balloons, however.

"Look, Beth! Look at those cool cars! I need one of those for my collection!" he tugged at his sister's arm as he pointed.

Elizabeth looked at the row of model cars lined up as prizes. "Do you think you can pop three balloons?" Elizabeth asked him.

"I don't know, but I'll sure try!" the boy said. Elizabeth

gave her brother a ticket, and James handed it to the man behind the counter.

While he was trying to pop the balloons, McKenzie leaned over and whispered, "It's getting late. We need to get back to the motel before ten so we can find the marbles."

Elizabeth couldn't hear her friend over the noise of the fair. "What?" she asked.

McKenzie repeated herself a little louder, but Elizabeth still couldn't hear. Finally, McKenzie ended up nearly shouting, "We've got to get back to the restaurant so we can look for the marbles!"

At that moment, Elizabeth spotted a tall flash of cowboy hat disappearing around the corner. She pointed, but the person was gone. "Was that—" Her question died. She decided she must be seeing things.

James popped one balloon but missed the other two. He was disappointed, and Elizabeth draped her arm over his shoulder. "It's okay, lil' brother. Come on. I see the house of mirrors. You'll love that!"

The four young people offered their tickets and entered. "We'll meet you at the exit," Mr. Phillips told them.

Inside, they giggled at the distorted images of themselves, some tall and wavy, others short and bumpy. They decided to chase each other through the maze, and before long, they were laughing and hollering. Each time they thought they'd caught one of the others, it turned out to be an image in the mirror!

Elizabeth began to see flashes of that cowboy hat again. Each time she focused on the image, it was gone. But then, there it was again, in the corner of her eye.

She told herself not to panic, but concentrated on finding the others. What in the world would Mr. Jacobs be doing in the house of mirrors? Was he shadowing them?

The Man in the Mirrors

"Hey y'all, I think we need to go. Everyone head for the exit," she called.

The others laughed. "Aww, you're not giving up that easily, are you?" called Evan.

Stay calm. Figure out how to get everyone out of here, away from that creepy cowboy, Elizabeth told herself. *Please, God, help.*

Then, she had an idea. "I'll race you! The last one to the exit is a rotten egg!" she called.

Within moments, she heard footsteps and hoots of laughter as the other three dashed to the exit. But then there was a thud, and the sound of something rolling on the floor. The marbles! Evan had kept them in his pocket!

"Oh, no! My marbles!" Elizabeth heard Evan calling out. She could see the images of marbles rolling on the floor but couldn't find them. Before long, she saw Evan's reflection. But everywhere she turned were more reflections. Where was the real thing?

"Here, let me help you with that," came a deep voice.

Elizabeth looked, and there was that cowboy hat, attached to Mr. Jacobs! And there he was again, and again, and again.

She had to find the real Evan and protect him from the real Mr. Jacobs!

She stood up, closed her eyes, and just listened to the voices, to the sounds of the marbles on the floor. Without opening her eyes, she turned toward the sound.

Holding her arms in front of her, she slowly began to walk, letting the sounds guide her. Before she knew it, she bumped into something. Opening her eyes, she looked directly down on a cowboy hat, sitting on top of Jacobs's head. The man was on his hands and knees, examining a handful of marbles. Evan was next to him, gathering more of the round balls.

"Here, let me help you," Elizabeth said, trying to keep her voice calm. Her heart was pounding, and she felt sure the others could hear its loud thud. Still, she kept her composure, knelt, and began searching.

"Hello, Elizabeth," said Mr. Jacobs.

Elizabeth forced herself not to look directly at the man. She tried to watch him in the mirrors as she looked for more marbles. "It's funny to see you here, Mr. Jacobs," Elizabeth said.

The man chuckled. "Aww, I'm just a big kid at heart. I love these fairs. I was supposed to meet Dan at the rodeo, to let him look at Lucy. But I thought I'd wander around the fair for a while first. Then I spotted you all over at the balloon darts. I've got something for your brother, by the way. I saw you kids come in here, and thought I'd try to catch up with you."

Elizabeth turned to look at the man. "If I didn't know better, I'd think you were following us," she said.

The cowboy chuckled. Was that a nervous laugh? "Well, I was starting to think you were following me," he said.

Elizabeth averted her eyes and called out to her friends again. "Meet everyone at the exit!" She stood, but found herself at a loss for which way to turn. *I really need to do something about my sense of direction, or lack of it,* she thought.

Mr. Jacobs stood and towered over her. Sensing her hesitancy, he said, "Follow me. I'll get you out of here."

Drats! She hated to depend on her prime suspect to get her unlost, but she didn't seem to have much choice. She kept her eyes fixed on the back of his plaid shirt, and before long, stepped into the bright lights of the fairground.

Mr. and Mrs. Phillips laughed when they saw Mr. Jacobs. "You're a brave man," Dan Phillips said.

Mr. Jacobs smiled but didn't make eye contact with anyone. Did he feel guilty about something? He reached into his pocket and pulled out a tiny model car. He handed it to James.

"I saw you trying to win a car, James. I thought you might like to have this," he said.

"Wow, thank you!" said James, a smile lighting his face. "And it's blue, too! My favorite color!"

Elizabeth and McKenzie exchanged glances. As the adults began talking and moving toward the rodeo grounds, the two girls stayed a few steps behind.

"What is he doing here?" Elizabeth whispered.

"He's meeting my dad, and they're going to look at that horse, remember?" McKenzie reminded her.

"Yeah, but it's strange that he seems to be following us. It's like he knows we know something," Elizabeth continued.

"Maybe. But I think it's a good idea for us to stay close to him anyway. We might learn something," McKenzie said.

The girls followed the rest of their group at a safe distance, so they could talk freely without fear of being heard.

"I wish the other Camp Club Girls were here. I think we need to e-mail them all tonight and see if we can get any more ideas," said McKenzie.

"That's it!" said Elizabeth. "Why didn't I think of that a long time ago? We can get them to help us investigate Mr. Jacobs!" She pulled her cell phone out of her pocket. Scrolling down in her address book, she hit Kate's number.

It was busy.

She moved to Sydney's number. After a couple of rings, Sydney's grandmother answered.

"Hello, Mrs. Washington. This is Elizabeth. How are you?" she asked politely.

"Oh, Elizabeth! What a nice surprise. I'm doing well, and you?"

"I'm fine, thank you, ma'am. May I please speak with Sydney?"

"Oh, she's not here. She's at a Wilderness Club meeting. She'll back in about an hour or so. Would you like me to have her call you back?"

"Oh, no thank you. I'll just e-mail her. Tell her I'm sorry I missed her."

"She will be so disappointed. I'll tell her you called. You take care now," said the woman.

Elizabeth hung up, and then sighed a frustrated sigh. McKenzie watched as she moved the arrow down to Alex's name and number, and pressed the button. It rang.

"Hello?" came Alex's voice from the other end of the line.

"Hi, Alex!" Elizabeth said.

"Elizabeth Anderson, is that you?" the girl exclaimed from the other end of the line.

"Yep, it is," replied Elizabeth.

"Is McKenzie with you? She better be. You e-mailed us all about your new mystery, and then it was like the two of you just dropped off the face of the earth. Haven't you been checking your e-mails?"

Elizabeth was surprised at Alex's scolding. She felt like

a child who had gotten caught sneaking a cookie. The truth was, Elizabeth and McKenzie had been too busy to think about e-mailing. "Uh. . .sorry," she said.

"You're forgiven," said Alex. "Now tell me everything! Did you find the jewels? Are Megan and her mother wealthy heiresses? Oh, this is *so* Hollywood! I can see it now. 'Impoverished woman inherits millions!' It will be made into a television movie, I just know it! You'll have your own mystery show. An *iCarly* on the go!"

Elizabeth held the phone away from her ear a bit. McKenzie could hear Alex's excited chatter from a couple of feet away. The two laughed. Same old Alex. She handed the phone to McKenzie, who said hello to her friend, then handed the phone back to Elizabeth.

"We haven't found the marbles yet. And Megan isn't exactly impoverished. But we need your help," she said.

"What can I do?" asked Alex.

"We couldn't find anything in our search for the marbles. But there is this cowboy named Mark Jacobs. He keeps snooping around. We know he's after the marbles, too. He claims to have inherited them from a rich uncle, but I think he's a fraud.

"We know a man named Foster left them to Megan's grandmother before she died. We're still trying to find where she might have hidden them. But can you check out Jacobs for us? And get the others in on the search, too. Mac and I are at the fair now, tailing the cowboy."

"Oh, how exciting! I wish I were there. I'll get right on it. I'll call you back if I find anything."

"Thanks, Alex." The two girls hurried to catch up with the rest of their group.

Mr. Jacobs and Mr. Phillips were talking, and the cowboy led them to a row of stalls where the horses waited to enter the rodeo arena. The announcer said something funny, and the crowd laughed.

"I ride again in about a half hour. Lucy has been a great horse. I hate to sell her, but at least I know she'll be in good hands."

"Tell me again why you're selling her," Mr. Phillips requested, and the girls scooted in closer, pretending to watch the rodeo. Evan and James were on the ground, driving the tiny car through tracks of loose hay.

"I'm ready to retire. The rodeo life is fun, but I want to put down roots somewhere. I don't have any family still living, but Amarillo was always special to my uncle, and I like it here, too. I've found a piece of land with a creek and a nice little house, and I want to settle here. I thought I had a sizable inheritance coming my way, but that doesn't seem to be panning out. So my backup plan has always been to sell my stock and supplies for a down payment."

"So if your inheritance comes through, you may not want to sell her?" asked Mr. Phillips.

Mr. Jacobs paused. "I hope my inheritance comes through, but I'm trying not to count on it. It's a long story," the cowboy said. His voice sounded so sad that Elizabeth couldn't help but look at him. When she did, she was surprised to see him looking at her! She looked away, but it was too late.

McKenzie's dad studied the horse, and Mrs. Phillips was talking to the boys. Jacobs stepped to the railing where the girls were leaning, and whispered, "I heard you talking to that waitress at the restaurant about some marbles. What kind of marbles are you looking for?"

Elizabeth couldn't believe her ears. Was the man really questioning her about the marbles? How could she get out of this conversation? Panicked, she looked at McKenzie, but Mac appeared as flustered as she felt.

Suddenly, the announcer's voice boomed over the loudspeaker. "We invite all of our young people, ages eight to fourteen, to enter the arena for the pig chase. You might get a little muddy, but you're sure to have a barrel of fun! The first one to catch a baby pig wins $250 cash."

McKenzie grabbed Elizabeth and pulled her into the arena. A woman at the gate attached a number to each contestant's back and instructed them to stand along the railing. Elizabeth looked at her new pink tennis shoes and knew they would never be the same.

"That was a close call," whispered Mac, as they waited

for the event to begin.

"Tell me about it! The nerve of that man, just coming out and asking me like that!"

"I feel sorry for him," said McKenzie. "He's all alone in the world, and now it looks like he'll have to sell his horse. I'd die if I had to sell mine."

Elizabeth looked at her friend in shock. "Don't tell me you're falling for his sob story! Don't let him fool you." Elizabeth tried to convince herself as much as she tried to convince her friend. Deep down, she shared McKenzie's sympathy. But he had to be a bad guy. He just had to be.

"Yeah, you're probably right," whispered McKenzie.

The gate closed, and the dozens of contestants were instructed to scatter throughout the arena. The announcer's voice said, "In just a moment, six piglets will be released into the arena. Oh, and did I mention they are covered in baby oil? When you hear the gunshot, you do whatever you can to catch one of these pigs. Of course, there will be no hitting or shoving or foul play of any kind, or you'll be disqualified. The first one to successfully catch and hold a pig wins the cash. Are you ready? Get set!"

The sound of a gunshot set the arena into chaos. Piglets raced into the arena, and the contestants sprang into action. The crowd roared with laughter and cheers. For a moment, Elizabeth stood frozen to her spot. She had never done anything like this!

McKenzie, on the other hand, was quite at home. She'd singled out a tiny black and white spotted pig and was trying to corner him. "Elizabeth, don't just stand there! Get moving!" she called out. "I could use a little help!"

Just then, a small pink blur ran over her foot, leaving behind tiny mud prints on her shoes. Elizabeth reached for the creature, but it was too late. She sprang forward to chase the offending animal. She could hear McKenzie calling her name, but Elizabeth had no interest in any other pig. This one had muddied her shoes. He was going to pay.

The pig ran around the arena, Elizabeth close at his heels. He led her through the center of the ring, around the outer edge, and into a mud puddle. In the background, she could hear James calling, "Go, Bettyboo! Go, Bettyboo!"

Suddenly, all of Elizabeth's frustrations took the form of the tiny piglet in front of her. She leaped forward in a stunning show of determination, grabbed the oily little creature, and held him to her chest. She wasn't about to let him escape.

The crowd stood to their feet and roared, and the announcer's voice exclaimed over the loudspeaker. "We have a winner! The pretty little blond, now covered in mud, has caught herself a pig! Folks, did you see her jump? She was determined to win that cash! Congratulations, miss!"

Elizabeth stayed where she was, her jeans soaking in the mud beneath her. She looked up to find McKenzie standing over her, hands on hips and a huge smile on her face.

"Congratulations! I didn't know you had it in you!" Mac told her.

"I didn't either," Elizabeth replied, as she gripped the wiggling animal in her arms.

A rodeo official approached and asked her name. The woman then spoke into a cordless microphone, "Our winner is Miss Elizabeth Anderson. Miss Anderson, on behalf of the Amarillo Livestock Show and Rodeo, we would like to present you with this certificate, and a check for $250. Congratulations!" She held out a large manila envelope as the crowd cheered.

Elizabeth still didn't move. She was afraid to let go of the pig, afraid he would escape.

The woman leaned forward and whispered, "You can let go now. You've already won."

Elizabeth laughed, then gave her wiggling bundle a kiss on the head and set him free. The crowd applauded as she stood to her feet and accepted the envelope. The contestants exited the arena, and the two girls were greeted by their group.

"Congratulations, Beth! Did you hear me cheering for you?" asked James.

Elizabeth took a muddy finger and smeared the tip of his nose. "Yes, I did, little brother. And your cheers helped me win!"

"We'd better get you home and out of those muddy clothes, Elizabeth," said Mrs. Phillips.

For the first time, Elizabeth noticed that McKenzie was as clean as a whistle. Not a mark on her, except for a little mud on her shoes. "How did you stay so clean?" she asked her friend.

"I guess I've had a little more experience than you," Mac laughed.

Then Mr. Jacobs clapped her on the back. In the excitement, Elizabeth had forgotten all about him! "That was great, Elizabeth. I have a feeling you're the kind of girl who always does what she sets out to do!"

Elizabeth shifted nervously from one foot to the other and looked at the ground. She wished the man would leave her alone. "Uh, I guess so," she whispered.

The man leaned in and whispered, "Whether it's catching a pig or solving a mystery, huh?"

Elizabeth jerked her head up and looked at him. The man winked at her and tipped his hat to the group. "I'll see you folks later," he said, and walked away.

A Fishy Clue

As they left the fair, the Phillipses stopped at the Andersons' house to drop James off and give Elizabeth a chance to change clothes. Then they returned to the motel, where the girls headed to the restaurant.

It was 9:45 when Jean Louise greeted the girls. There were still a few scattered customers. "Take a seat, girls, and mind your manners 'til all the customers are gone," the woman told them.

They sat under the blue marlin. "I'm itching to take that thing off the wall and look behind it! I know we'll find the marbles there," said McKenzie.

Elizabeth's eyes lit with excitement. "I do, too. Hey, what if they are actually inside the fish? Maybe it's hollow!"

The girls continued whispering until it looked like the last customer had left. Just as Jean Louise was about to lock the door, it pushed open, and Mr. Jacobs walked in! Had he been looking for them again?

He looked around, tipping his hat to the girls before greeting Jean Louise. "Pardon me, ma'am. I know it's closing time, but could I trouble you for a tall glass of that wonderful iced tea?"

"Why certainly. I'll get it for you right now," said the waitress.

While he waited, he looked at the girls. "Fancy meeting you here," he said. "What are you girls doing here so late?"

Elizabeth looked like a deer caught in the headlights. She had no idea how to respond.

McKenzie, thinking fast, eyed the grand piano sitting in the corner of the restaurant. "Uh, Elizabeth plays the piano. Since she's spent the week here, with me, she's hardly gotten to practice. So she's going to practice after everyone leaves."

"That's right. Elizabeth's going to play the piano. Here's your tea, sir," said Jean Louise, handing the man a large Styrofoam cup. Megan had followed her out of the kitchen and had a towel draped over her shoulder.

"I see. I'd love to stay and listen. Would you mind?" the man said.

Elizabeth looked at Mac, then at the old piano. Taking a deep breath, she walked across the room and sat at the bench. Mr. Jacobs dropped into one of the booths and watched. *Why won't he just go away?* she thought. *I don't like to play in front of anybody, and especially not sneaky, low-down cowboys!*

She began to play Mozart's Sonata in C, and then transitioned into a praise song. Before long, she became absorbed in her music, and she played nearly flawlessly for the next several minutes. By the time she had finished, she had almost forgotten anyone else was in the room. She was startled by their applause and cheers, and began to blush.

"I'm impressed," said Jacobs. "Not very many people have a gift like that. 'I will sing and make music to the Lord,' Psalm 27:6."

"Thank you," she whispered, and turned back to the keyboard. *Now he's quoting scripture?* Elizabeth had no idea what to make of this man.

He stood to his feet and tipped his hat. "Thank you for the tea, and for the music. Good night, ladies," he told them, and walked out the door.

As soon as he was out of sight, the girls all sighed with relief. "What are we going to do?" Elizabeth asked. "He's following us. He knows we're on to something."

Jean Louise stopped smacking her gum and said, "You do the only thing you can do. You keep looking, and you beat him to the treasure. Come on, ladies. Let's tear this place apart!"

Megan climbed on the table and hefted the large fish off the wall. The four of them examined it, but didn't find any secret compartments or hollow spots. They looked at the wall behind the fish. They examined the floor beneath the fish. They even moved all the booths and benches to make sure there was nothing hidden beneath them.

"What if they're hidden in the stuffing of one of the benches?" Elizabeth asked. She was about ready to tear into a bench with a steak knife when Jean Louise stopped her.

"Whoa, there. This furniture gets replaced every ten years or so. If Emily Marie hid the marbles in one of the benches, they are long gone by now."

Frustrated, the girls sank into one of the booths. Megan looked close to tears as she said, "We might as well hang it up. We'll never find those marbles."

Elizabeth wanted to argue, but she was feeling the same way. Then, she remembered her prize money.

"Megan, do you know what I did tonight before I came here?" Elizabeth asked.

"I don't know. What?"

"I caught a pig," Elizabeth said with a giggle.

Megan sat up, and said, "You did what?" She looked to McKenzie for confirmation.

"She did," Mac told her. "She caught a pig at the Livestock Show and Rodeo, in front of the entire stadium. And she was covered from head to toe in mud!"

"You're kidding!" Megan laughed at the thought. "You mean Miss Perfect, always-keeps-her-room-clean, never-a-hair-out-of-place Elizabeth was covered in mud?"

"Yep. And she won the prize, too," Mac said.

"Really? What was the prize?" asked Megan.

"It's money. Not much, but I already know how I'm going

to spend it," said Elizabeth. "I'm going to buy a saxophone."

"A saxophone?" the two girls asked in unison.

"I didn't know you wanted to play the saxophone," said Megan.

"I don't. But I would love to have someone accompany me on the saxophone. Me on the piano. . .you know. A duet," Elizabeth said.

Slowly, Megan realized that Elizabeth wanted to purchase her band instrument for her. "Elizabeth, I can't let you do that."

"Why not? It's my money. I'll spend it however I want," Elizabeth told her.

They were interrupted by Jean Louise. "Girls, I promised your parents I'd have you all home before midnight, and it's almost that time now. We'd better go."

They piled into the woman's car, and within minutes they were pulling up to Elizabeth's house where the girls were going to spend the night. They were surprised to see the lights still on. "Thanks, Jean Louise!" they called from the porch. The woman waved and drove away.

Inside, Elizabeth's mom, dad, and brother were in the living room. James was chattering a mile a minute about spooky houses and greasy pigs and somebody losing marbles. Between sentences, he zoomed the tiny blue car through the air.

"Why are y'all still awake?" Elizabeth asked.

"Someone had too much cotton candy," her mother nodded to James. "Besides, we wanted to make sure you girls made it home safely."

"Can anyone explain to us what the spooky house is?" asked Mr. Anderson. James was still zooming his car around the room.

"Probably the house of mirrors. Evan's marbles spilled out of his pocket while we were in there."

Mr. and Mrs. Anderson burst into laughter. "So that's what he was talking about when he said Evan lost his marbles! We thought Evan had gone crazy!"

The girls giggled, and the adults stood. "There are snacks in the kitchen, girls. Try not to stay up too late. James, it is way past your bedtime. Come on. Into bed you go."

James obeyed, still zooming his tiny blue Cadillac as he headed down the hallway toward his room. "This is the coolest car I've ever seen. Just look at those fins!"

The girls looked at one another in stunned excitement. "Fins!" they all three called out at once. "The Cadillac Ranch!"

•—•—•

Within the next half hour, e-mails were flying. Alexis had contacted the other Camp Club Girls, and they were expecting Elizabeth and McKenzie to be online around midnight.

Elizabeth's fingers clicked away at the keyboard: *We searched the restaurant. No luck. We wonder if the marbles are hidden at the Cadillac Ranch. Did anyone find information on Mark Jacobs?*

Bailey: *The only thing I found on your Roy Rogers is that he's an award-winning rodeo rider. I found his picture, too. You're right! He is handsome.*

Elizabeth: *We can't figure the guy out. One minute he's following us and asking questions. Then he quotes scripture. Either he's a really nice guy, or he's a great crook. I guess we'll see what happens at the Cadillac Ranch tomorrow.*

Kate: *Too Bad u can't attach a secret spy camera or recorder to him to see what he's doing and saying when you aren't around. That might help.*

Sydney: *What are you going to do? Just go there and start digging? You might get arrested.*

McKenzie took over the keyboard: *Well what else can we do? Any suggestions?*

Alexis: *What led you to the Cadillac Ranch? I thought we were looking for fins, or something. I'm confused.*

Mac typed out the events of the evening, including James's exclamation over his car's fins.

McKenzie: *We plan to visit there tomorrow. I guess we'll look around and see what we can find. Maybe we'll have to go back after dark.*

The girls all signed off, promising to do further research and stay in close contact.

During this time, Megan sat quietly at the kitchen table,

observing the exchange. "You need to take a shovel with you tomorrow. I'll be working—as usual."

"How can we take a shovel without everyone seeing it?" asked McKenzie.

Elizabeth eyed the pot of geraniums on the kitchen windowsill. "We can't take a full-sized shovel. But I know what we can take." She stood up and walked to the back door. Flipping on the porch light, she stepped outside.

McKenzie and Megan looked at each other and shrugged their shoulders. They could hear Elizabeth rummaging around on the porch. Finally, they heard their friend call out, "Got it!"

Elizabeth walked back into the kitchen holding a garden spade. "It may take us a while, but this will definitely dig a hole. Trust me. I've dug plenty of holes with this for my mom's garden."

"That's a great idea, Beth, but Sydney is right. We can't just go out there in broad daylight and dig."

The three girls sat drumming their fingers on the table, trying to think of a solution. "We've got to get out there in the evening when there aren't so many tourists. But how?"

Megan sat up straight. "We could ride our bikes. It's only a couple of miles outside of town."

"Do you know how to get there?" Elizabeth asked her.

"Yeah," the older girl answered. "I even know a shortcut from the church."

"Mac can ride my bike, and I'll ride my mom's," said Elizabeth.

"We've just got to figure out a reason to go to the church tomorrow evening, since it's not a church night," said McKenzie.

"That'll be easy," Megan told her. "Elizabeth's family practically lives at the church, anyway."

The girls talked a little longer, but their conversation was interrupted by yawns. Before long, the three young detectives scooted to bed.

•—•—•

The next morning, the girls slept in. The sun was high in the sky by the time Elizabeth woke to a paper airplane landing on her face. She fluttered her eyes and found James staring at her.

"Mama said to get up if you want to go to the Cadillac Ranch. McKenzie's parents will be here in a little while to pick us up."

Elizabeth rolled over and pulled the covers over her head, but James was persistent.

"Mama said if you get up now, she'll make homemade doughnuts. But if you wait too long, you'll only get cereal."

McKenzie popped up from her pallet on the floor.

"Homemade doughnuts? I love doughnuts," she said sleepily.

Megan stirred from her sleeping bag, and said, "Tell

your mom we'll be there in a minute, James."

James jumped from his spot on Elizabeth's bed, and she heard him padding down the hallway. Groaning, she forced herself to sit up.

The girls looked at each other, each one wanting a hot doughnut, but none wanting to actually leave bed.

McKenzie finally spoke. "Tomorrow is our last full day here. We go home the next day."

Elizabeth groaned and flopped back down in her bed. "I don't want to think about it. I've gotten used to having you around twenty-four hours a day."

"Y'all, we've got to find those marbles," Megan said, rummaging around in her bag and pulling out her toothbrush.

"Let's review the plan. We'll ride our bikes to the church this evening. And you know a shortcut from there to the Cadillac Ranch?" Elizabeth asked.

Megan nodded.

"It sounds like the perfect plan," said McKenzie. "So why do I have a bad feeling about the whole thing?"

"Riding our bikes two miles out of town doesn't sound great to me, either," said Elizabeth. "But sometimes you've just got to do what you've got to do. And we've got to find those marbles before Mr. Jacobs does."

James banged on the door, hollering, "Mama says come now while the doughnuts are hot!"

"We're coming!" Elizabeth called back. Then she said, "Let's just take this one step at a time. We're going out there today. Maybe we'll be able to dig some. Let's see what happens."

Nodding, the girls stood up and followed the smell of fresh, hot doughnuts.

•—•—•

Elizabeth and McKenzie stared at the row of Cadillacs, noses buried in the ground, tails sticking high in the air. "Cadillac Ranch my foot. This is a Cadillac graveyard!" McKenzie said.

Elizabeth giggled. "Who would think of doing such a thing?"

"Apparently, Chip Lord, Hudson Marquez, and Doug Michaels," Mac replied, referring to the brochure she held. "They are supposed to represent the birth and death of the early model Cadillacs, and an era in American culture. They are buried at the same angle as the Great Pyramid of Giza, in Egypt."

"Groovy," responded Elizabeth, and Mac giggled at the old-fashioned word.

The sun glistened off the shiny metal, and the girls shielded their eyes from the glare. Evan and James were already running in and out of the cars, exclaiming over the bright colors and shapes.

"Well, there's the blue one, third from the end," said

Elizabeth. "We might as well take a look."

The girls smiled as they passed another group of tourists. "We'll never get to explore with all these people around taking pictures at every turn," whispered McKenzie.

Elizabeth fingered the garden spade in her purse as they approached the blue Cadillac. "I have an idea. Stand in front of me, and I'll kneel down like I'm inspecting the motor. Watch for people, and tell me when anyone is coming."

McKenzie did as she was told, exclaiming loudly over different features of the car every time a tourist walked by. At one point, she even posed for a picture one of them was snapping.

"What are you doing?" Elizabeth asked her.

"Hiding in plain sight," Mac answered.

"Huh?" Elizabeth grunted, confused.

"If it looks like we're trying to hide what we're doing, people will be suspicious. But if we just act like goofy tourists, no one will suspect a thing!" Mac explained.

"Mac, you don't have to act like a goofy tourist. You are one," Elizabeth said with a laugh.

"Just keep digging," ordered Mac, and Elizabeth obeyed.

All of a sudden, she hit something in the dirt. Something hard. "Mac! I think I've found it!" she whispered.

Mrs. Phillips chose that moment to call, "Girls! Come on. We have several more stops to make today."

Mac stiffened and told Elizabeth, "Quick! Cover it up! My mom's coming over here. We'll have to come back tonight."

Elizabeth frantically replaced the dirt in the hole she'd dug, and slipped the spade back into her purse as Mrs. Phillips approached. "You two sure are fascinated with this blue one. Hey look, Elizabeth, it matches your eyes. I'll tell your dad he needs to buy you a blue car one day."

Elizabeth laughed and replied, "A blue *Cadillac.*"

Mrs. Phillips chuckled and began moving toward the car. The two secret sleuths took deep breaths, gave one last look over their shoulders at the loose dirt beneath the motor of the car, and followed her.

Danger in the Dark!

That evening, the girls sat in the Andersons' kitchen acting bored. Mrs. Anderson was putting the last dish in the dishwasher.

"I need to get some exercise," said McKenzie. "All this vacationing and lounging around the pool is making me tired."

"Why don't we ride bikes?" Elizabeth asked.

"That sounds great. But I don't have my bicycle here."

"Why don't you ride mine? That is, if my dear mother will let me ride hers," Elizabeth said, smiling at her mom.

Mrs. Anderson smiled. "That sounds like a wonderful idea. It's a beautiful evening for a bike ride."

"I have an idea. Mom, I left my library book at church last Sunday. Can we ride up there to get it?"

"I suppose. Just stay on the back roads. Don't go in the busy streets," she said. "And why don't you ask Megan to go, too. She needs to get out more."

Within minutes, the plan was underway. The three girls rode their bikes the short distance to the church. When Megan led them on a narrow trail behind the church,

Elizabeth said, "What about my library book? We need to stop and get it."

"We'll stop on the way back," Megan called over her shoulder. "Let's get out there while we still have some light. The church doors will still be open 'til at least ten. I think the senior high teens are having a volleyball tournament or something there tonight."

"This is so exciting," said Mac. "I can't believe we're actually going to find the marbles."

"We *hope* we're going to find the marbles," Elizabeth corrected. "But I do have a good feeling about this. Something was down there this afternoon when I was digging. And that's the last place your grandmother was, Megan, before she got in the car wreck. Remember, she was serving at a party there so it would have been easy for her to step outside and hide them there. "

The bike trail grew bumpy, and tall ears of corn formed a wall on either side of them.

"Uh, Megs, are you sure you know where you're going?" asked Elizabeth.

"Trust me. It's just a little further," she called over her shoulder.

Sure enough, a few minutes later they pulled into a clearing. Ahead of them was the row of cars, half buried in the ground.

"I had no idea this was so close," said Elizabeth.

"Yeah," agreed McKenzie. "It seemed a lot farther in the car today."

"It is farther when you take the main road. That's why they call it a shortcut!"

The girls stowed their bikes in the tall stalks of corn and surveyed the field before them.

With whispers and giggles of excitement, they started digging through their backpacks, pulling out supplies.

"Where's the other flashlight?" whispered Megan.

"I have it," Mac answered, clicking on the beam.

"Turn it off. You'll run the battery down. We don't need it yet," Megan whispered, and McKenzie turned it off.

"I have the spade and another small shovel," whispered Elizabeth. Then, as an afterthought, she asked, "Why are we whispering? No one is around."

The girls giggled nervously. "I don't know. It just feels like we're supposed to be whispering," answered Mac. The three made their way across the country field to where the ten Cadillacs stood with their rear ends sticking in the air.

Stopping in front of the blue one, they found the place where Elizabeth had dug that afternoon.

"Here it is," Mac whispered. "Megan, you've been working all day. You keep watch while Elizabeth and I dig."

"Okay," the sixteen-year-old answered. Something in her face held a look of hope that made her look much younger than the other two. "Please, God, let the marbles be here."

"I'm surprised they don't have more security here," McKenzie said.

"Why? They're just a bunch of junk cars," Elizabeth pointed out.

"But they could still be vandalized," McKenzie said as she started to dig.

"Guess they're not too concerned," Elizabeth said.

Elizabeth and Mac moved the loose dirt to the side and found the hard object Elizabeth had felt earlier. With grunts and groans, they pulled the object out of its resting place.

"A rock," they all three sighed with disappointment.

"Let's keep digging," Elizabeth said, and she and Mac went back to work. They dug and dug, finding nothing. Finally, sweat dripping down her brow, Elizabeth realized she had a problem.

"Uh, y'all?"

"Yeah?" the other two answered.

"Remember that soda I drank earlier?"

"Yeah?" they answered again.

"Remember the refill?"

"Uh-huh," came the reply.

"I have to go to the bathroom."

Mac giggled, and Megan sighed.

"I really have to go. Now!"

"Well, go! Nobody can see you," Megan told her.

"I'm not going to the bathroom right here! That's disgusting!" Elizabeth said.

"You could go back to where we parked the bikes," Mac suggested. "But then again, that might be too corny!" She laughed at her own joke, and the other girls snickered.

Elizabeth crossed her legs. "It's getting dark," she whispered.

Mac and Megan kept working.

"Will somebody go with me?"

"No," they both responded.

"Here, take the big flashlight. Mac and I will stay here with the smaller one. Hurry back," Megan said, handing her the larger of the two lights.

Elizabeth dashed toward the direction of the bikes. Only she couldn't actually see the bikes, and there were several little trails that led off the field. She didn't know which one to take. Soon, she couldn't wait any longer, and just followed one of the trails a few feet from the opening. Turning around, she could still see her friends' flashlight beam, and knew she could find her way back to them. Shining her light, she found a place that seemed to offer enough privacy, and took care of her business.

Suddenly, a flash of headlights flooded the area, and she ducked behind the corn. Her breath caught in her throat as she watched the pickup truck pass on the road in front of the cars and saw the silhouette of the driver, wearing a cowboy hat.

Mr. Jacobs!

Had Megan and Mac seen? She had to warn them! But their flashlight beam had disappeared. Where had they gone? Had they seen the headlights, too?

The truck pulled to the side of the road. Its headlights lit up the small gate before they died down. She heard the sound of the truck door opening. Closing. The beam of another flashlight clicked on.

The new flashlight steadily moved toward the row of upturned cars! She watched, not knowing where to go or what to do. Turning around, she realized she was lost. She had no idea where the bikes were. And the sun had disappeared from the horizon.

The night was black, except for her flashlight.

It can't be too far, she thought. *I think I need to go. . . this way.* Staying low behind the corn stalks, she cupped her hand around her flashlight beam. *Maybe this will keep Jacobs from spotting me.*

Dear God, she prayed, *this was a stupid idea. What were we thinking? Riding out here alone at night. . . God, I'm scared. Please be with Megan and Mac, and keep them safe. And please help me to find my way back to them!*

She looked toward the old cars. Only one beam of light. She knew by its brightness it belonged to Mr. Jacobs—the girls had kept the tiny light for themselves. "Where are they?" she whispered. Suddenly, the clouds shifted. The moon cast a soft glow on the area.

Then, a rustling sound! She put her fist in her mouth to keep from gasping.

"Elizabeth?" Megan's whisper came through the darkness.

"Meg? Where are you? I got turned around, and I can't find the bikes!" Elizabeth whispered back.

A tiny beam of light flickered on and off, and Elizabeth scooted toward it. She saw the shapes of her two friends, and she let out the breath she hadn't known she was holding. Sliding onto her bike, she commanded, "Let's get out of here!"

The girls pedaled faster and faster, away from the Cadillac Ranch, away from danger. Corn husks slapped their faces and ankles. Elizabeth nearly lost her balance on the bumpy trail, but she kept going.

No one said a word until they approached the lights of the church. The only sounds were the tires on the rough road, and the girls' heavy breathing.

Elizabeth spoke first. "What happened back there? I was so scared!"

Mac turned around on her seat. "A couple of minutes after you left, we saw the truck's headlights coming up the road. We thought it would just pass, but we turned off our flashlight just in case. Then, when it stopped, we knew we had to get out of there!"

"We hoped you'd be at the bikes when we got there, but I should have known better. How could you have gotten lost? It's a bare field. Nothing's there!" Megan teased her friend.

"You know how easily I get turned around. When I saw him stop the truck, and then I couldn't find y'all, I just about died. I was so scared!"

"So were we!" Megan and Mac replied.

"When we turned our flashlight off, we couldn't see a thing! Then the clouds shifted, and the moon gave us just enough light to find our way back to the bikes. But you weren't there," Megan continued.

Elizabeth felt a warm feeling and knew that God had sent that moonlight as an answer to her prayer. Then, she remembered their reason for going out there in the first place. "Did you find the marbles?" she asked.

Megan kept her eyes on the road but said nothing. Mac silently shook her head.

As they turned onto the street that Elizabeth and Megan called home, they were surprised to see five adults standing in the driveway. None of them looked happy.

Elizabeth watched relief cover her mother's face, and she realized they had been out longer than they'd realized.

"Where have you girls been? It got dark half an hour ago! We've been worried sick!" exclaimed Ruby Smith, first hugging her daughter and then giving her a frustrated look.

The other two sets of parents reached for their own daughters. "You girls had better have a good explanation," McKenzie's father told them.

"Why don't we go inside? I have a feeling this is going to take a while," said Mr. Anderson.

The three girls filed into the living room, followed by the adults. Evan was sound asleep on the sofa, and Elizabeth assumed James was down the hall, in his own bed.

"Let's go in the kitchen. I'll make some coffee," suggested Mrs. Anderson. The adults sat around the table, leaving the three girls to lean against the counter.

"We're ready when you are. Spill it," said Ruby Smith, looking at her daughter.

Megan took a deep breath, and said, "Mom, those marbles are real. And Mark Jacobs is after them. He's been looking for them this whole time, and I think he knows they belong to you and Uncle Jack. You work so hard all the time, and I just thought—"

"That's what this is about? Those silly marbles? Megan Rebecca Smith, I ought to tan your hide! That is the most ridiculous—"

"Excuse me, Ruby, but what's this about Mark Jacobs? He seems like a decent man to me," said Mr. Phillips. He looked to McKenzie. "Would you like to tell me what's going on?"

McKenzie looked at her father, and said, "I'm sorry, Daddy. But we think he's a con man. Megan's mother inherited some jewels, but she didn't know it. Now Jacobs is trying to get them before she does."

"Jewels?" he asked. "Megan said you were looking for marbles!"

"Hold on a minute," Elizabeth's father interrupted. "I think we'd better back up and start from the beginning. Elizabeth, why don't you start?"

It took a lot of starting and stopping, but eventually the adults were filled in on the entire account. It was late, and the adults decided to withhold judgment until the next day. McKenzie cast Elizabeth a worried look over her shoulder as she stepped onto the front porch.

Megan kept her head down as she followed her mother to their own front door. When everyone was gone, Elizabeth turned to face her parents. She hated the disappointment she read there.

"We'll talk about this in the morning. There is cold pizza in the refrigerator, if you're hungry. Get a snack, and go to bed," her father told her, and then joined her mother in their own bedroom. She could hear them talking but couldn't make out any words as she poured herself a glass of milk. She tried to drink it, but the knot in her throat made it difficult to swallow. She was about to place the glass back in the refrigerator when she noticed the e-mail light flashing at the bottom of the computer screen.

Sitting at the desk, she opened her inbox. There was a message from Kate. It read:

Did some research. The Cadillac Ranch has moved. Is now in a different location than it was 30 years ago.

You're looking in the wrong place.

The next morning, Elizabeth sat at the kitchen table with her parents, listening to the lecture she knew she deserved. "I can't believe you girls rode out there at night, alone. Why didn't you come to us?"

Elizabeth tried to explain. "I know it was a dumb thing to do. I can't even begin to tell you how sorry I am. I know there's no excuse, but I was only thinking of Megan and her mom. They've had such a hard time since Mr. Smith died, and these marbles would help them so much. And I guess I was afraid you wouldn't take the whole thing seriously."

Her mom and dad looked at one another, then back at her. "Maybe you're right. We might not have taken this seriously," her mom said. "We still see you as our little girl, playing make-believe. But Elizabeth, you can always come to us about anything. There's no excuse for what you did last night."

Elizabeth looked at her hands. She was truly sorry for sneaking around behind their backs.

Her dad spoke up then. "First you sneaked out of your window, in a storm. Then, you go riding off without telling us where you are. At night! Anything could have happened. I know your intentions were good, but that's no excuse for acting foolish. You're grounded to the house for the next two weeks. But we won't start the punishment until after McKenzie goes home. We know you want to spend as much time with her as possible."

Elizabeth scooted her chair back and threw her arms around her parents' necks. "Thank you so much! I promise I'll never do anything like that ever again!" Then, remembering Kate's e-mail, she said, "Uh, Mom and Dad? There's one more thing I need to talk to you about." She shared the latest discovery, only to be interrupted by her father.

"That's right. I had forgotten about them moving the Cadillac Ranch. I know exactly where it used to be."

"Really?" Elizabeth questioned. "Will you take us there?"

He smiled at his daughter and said, "Of course I will. But it's not that simple. The old location was in a huge wheat field. Trying to find your marbles there would be like looking for a needle in a haystack."

"Dad, you do the driving and leave the rest to me," she told him. Sitting down at the computer, she typed *Cadillac Ranch—original location—pictures* into the search engine.

Sure enough, dozens of pictures popped up. Elizabeth knew she was on the brink of discovery when she noticed something. In each of the pictures, the Cadillacs were painted differently. Some of the pictures even had graffiti covering each of the cars. How in the world was she supposed to figure out which one was the blue one?

She let out a groan just as the phone rang. "Hello?" she spoke into the receiver.

"Elizabeth? It's Mac. Are you in as much trouble as I am?"

"I'm grounded for two weeks. But Mom and Dad said it

can wait until after you leave."

"That's good. We leave tomorrow, and I'd hate it if we couldn't spend my last day together. But I have bad news."

Elizabeth braced herself for whatever Mac had to say. But she never would have guessed just how bad that news was. . .

The Best Vacation Ever

"This morning when I woke up, I heard voices outside our door. I peeked out the window, and my dad was out there talking to Mr. Jacobs. And he was showing him the journals."

Elizabeth nearly dropped the phone. "He what?" she croaked. Visions of the tall cowboy, riding off into the sunset holding the bag of marbles flashed through her mind. "Why would he do such a thing?"

McKenzie sighed. "He's convinced that Jacobs is a nice guy. Even after hearing the whole story."

Elizabeth took a deep breath. "Well, we can't do anything about it now. But Mac, listen. After y'all left last night, I had an e-mail from Kate. The Cadillac Ranch has changed locations! We weren't even digging at the right site!"

"You're kidding," said McKenzie with a groan. "What will we do?"

"My dad said he'd take us out there today. I've got pictures of where the cars used to be, but they've been painted over the years. I'll do some more research. Do you think your parents will let you come?"

"I don't know. Let me call you back."

"Okay, but hurry. We've got to get there before Mr. Jacobs does," Elizabeth told her.

Within the hour, the Andersons, Phillipses, and Smiths were all squeezed into the Andersons' van. Heavy, dark clouds were moving in, giving a sense of urgency to the situation.

"The storm looks a ways away. I think we can beat it," Mr. Phillips said. Elizabeth's dad started the car, and they headed toward the old Cadillac Ranch.

Elizabeth, McKenzie, and Megan sat in the backseat of the van. Elizabeth had printed some pictures so they could get an idea of the location. She had even found a picture dated close to the time of Emily Marie's death.

"Why are the cars different colors in the pictures?" asked Megan.

"The cars are repainted every so often. Once, they were all painted pink, in support of breast cancer victims. Tourists are allowed—even encouraged, to paint graffiti on the cars, and every so often they are repainted to offer a fresh canvas," Elizabeth told them.

"So we have no way of knowing which car was blue at the time of my grandmother's death?" asked Megan.

"Not really. This picture is dated the same year, and the blue car is the fourth from the right. Look, it's lined up with this telephone pole, and there are two big oak trees in the background, one on either side of it. Hopefully, the telephone pole and the trees are still there," Elizabeth said.

Before long, Mr. Anderson stopped the car on the edge of an endless wheat field. "This will be tough," murmured McKenzie.

Everyone piled out of the car, and immediately James and Evan began chasing one another in and out of the rows of wheat.

Elizabeth looked at her father. "How will we ever do this?" she asked him.

"This is your job. Remember, you said all I had to do was drive." Patting her on the shoulder, he whispered, "I have faith in you."

Elizabeth stood a little taller and held the pictures to the horizon. "Okay, girls, it looks like it's up to us. First things first. Let's find these trees."

Before they knew it, everyone was hunting—even James and Evan. The pictures were passed from person to person, with cries of, "There's a tree!" and "Look! There's an electrical pole!"

They were all distracted with their scavenger hunt and didn't notice a beat-up truck pulling up behind them. An old farmer got out and asked, "Can I help you folks with somethin'?"

Mr. Anderson stepped forward and shook the man's

hand. "Yes, sir, there is. We're looking for the original location of the Cadillac Ranch."

The man scratched his head and chuckled. "Well, there's not much to see. But I can take you to it if you'd like," he said.

Elizabeth and McKenzie started jumping up and down. "Really? You'll take us to the exact spot?"

The old farmer shook his head and muttered, "Crazy tourists." He got in his truck, rolled down his window, and said, "Follow me."

A crash of thunder sounded, and the group piled in the car just as the first drops of rain started falling from the sky. The man led them to a spot about a half mile up the road, and veered off to the left. Rolling the window down, he pointed to a sign, half covered with wheat. It read, "ORIGINAL LOCATION OF THE CADILLAC RANCH." Small posts stuck out of the ground, to show where each car had stood. The man waved and drove away.

"I don't believe it," Megan whispered.

Thank You, God, Elizabeth prayed silently. *Please let us find the jewels. Marbles. Whatever they are, Lord, please help us find them.*

The three girls climbed out of the van, but the adults didn't want to get wet. Mr. Phillips handed McKenzie a shovel through the open window. They were splattering through the mud when they realized Ruby Smith was on their heels.

"I'm going to help. If those marbles are real, I want to be there when they are found," the woman told them.

Elizabeth smiled, reached into her purse, and handed her the spade.

They located the fourth post from the right and started digging. The rain softened the earth, making the digging easier. And messier.

Thunder continued crashing, but the four females paid no attention. They were so focused on their task that they didn't notice a large pair of mud-covered cowboy boots approaching.

"May I give you a hand?" Mark Jacobs's voice spoke over the sound of the rain.

Startled, Ruby looked up at him and continued digging. The three girls weren't sure how to respond to his presence and stopped what they were doing.

Gently, the man took the large shovel from McKenzie and started digging on the opposite side of the post. His muscles took the shovel deeper into the ground than the girls had been able to dig, and after a couple of scoops, the shovel revealed an old, small tin cashbox. Ruby's mouth dropped open, and she looked up at the man.

"I bet this belongs to you," he said.

The woman reached down and took the box from the shovel. Her mud-covered hands shook as she opened it. Inside was a velvet bag. Inside that were some papers and a smaller cloth bag with a drawstring tie.

By this time, Elizabeth's and McKenzie's parents had joined them. No one spoke as Ruby Smith opened the bag her mother had buried so long ago. She emptied its contents into her hands, and twelve of the most beautiful, brightly colored marbles spilled out.

"Oh!" the woman cried. "Oh, Mama!"

Megan knelt in the mud beside her mother and hugged her as they both wept.

The rest of the group decided to give them privacy and headed back to the van. Jacobs turned to go, but Ruby called out, "Wait! I have so many questions. Where are you going?"

The tall cowboy smiled and said, "We'll have plenty of time to talk later. Right now, you enjoy this moment with your daughter and her friends." He tipped his hat and left.

Without warning, the rain stopped, and the sun broke through the clouds. The marbles in Ruby's hands cast a brilliant glow on her face as she looked at her daughter. "We're going to be okay," she whispered.

•—•—•

The group sat around the table at the Big Texan Steak Ranch, drinking in the exchange between Ruby Smith and Mark Jacobs. Even Jean Louise, who was their waitress, had broken the rules and pulled a chair up to the table.

"I can't believe Foster Wilson was your uncle. I never

met him, though I do remember Mama talking about a nice man she wanted me and Jack to meet," Ruby told the man sitting across from her.

"It's as much of a surprise to me as it is to you. I always knew Uncle Foster fell in love here in Amarillo. I just never knew the whole story," Mr. Jacobs responded. He looked around the table, and his eyes rested on Elizabeth. "I knew you were on to me, and I'm sorry I made you nervous. When I realized you were after the same thing I was, I just figured you were some detective wannabe. You were always one step ahead of me, though. When I figured out you really knew what you were doing, I began to follow you. Sorry if I scared you."

"That's okay. I'm sorry I thought you were a con m—"

"Elizabeth!" her mother stopped her.

Mr. Jacobs tilted his head back and roared. "It's okay, Sue. She had every right to believe I was a con man."

Everyone laughed this time. Then Ruby spoke again.

"I've given this a lot of thought, Mark, and my brother, Jack, and I have talked about it on the phone. He agrees with me, and I don't want to hear any arguments. There are twelve marbles, and we're going to split them. Jack and I will take six and the other six belong to you," Ruby said.

"Oh, no, Ruby, I couldn't, now that I know the whole story. Those were a gift to your mother. I wouldn't dream of taking them," Jacobs replied.

"Now Mark Jacobs, you listen. Your uncle would have wanted you to have them as much as he wanted me to have them. You can argue with me all you want, but I'll get my way. Each marble is worth close to one hundred thousand dollars. We can certainly afford to share them," Ruby argued.

Jacobs opened his mouth, but Ruby cut him off. "Not another word!" she said.

The handsome cowboy leaned back in his chair and grinned. "How do you know what I was going to say?" he asked.

"You were going to argue with me, I know that," the woman told him.

"No, ma'am. I know better than to argue with you; I have the feeling that once your mind is made up, there's no changing it."

"You're right about that," Ruby told him. The two bantered back and forth as if no one else were in the room.

McKenzie nudged Elizabeth under the table, then whispered, "I don't know why she's giving him the marbles. When they get married, they'll belong to both of them."

The two girls giggled. "Let's not rush things," Elizabeth whispered back. "But they do make a nice couple, don't they?"

They turned their attention back to Ruby and the cowboy. "So, what were you going to say?" Ruby asked coyly.

Jacobs looked her in the eye and said, "I was going to say that I came here looking for a treasure. I believe I may have found one, whose worth is far more than rubies. And her name. . .is Ruby."

The group applauded, then Jean Louise began taking their orders.

Elizabeth focused her attention on Megan, who was smiling and watching her mother. "You look happy," she told her friend.

Megan turned to Elizabeth and McKenzie. "It just feels so good to see Mom smile. It's been a long time since I've seen her so happy. And it's all thanks to the two of you and the Camp Club Girls."

Elizabeth glanced at Megan's mom, laughing at something Jacobs had said. "I'm not sure if we can take the credit for making your mom smile. I think that goes to a certain handsome cowboy," she told her friend.

Megan laughed. "He may have something to do with it, but the sadness is gone from her face. Now, she won't have to work so hard all the time. Now, she doesn't have to worry as much about paying the bills every month. And I owe it all to the two of you and your excellent sleuthing skills."

"I just wish we didn't have to leave as soon as we finish our lunch here," said McKenzie. Then, reaching into her backpack she said, "Oh! Before I forget. . .these belong to Jean Louise."

She pulled out the journals. Then she turned again to

Megan. "Thank you for letting me help solve the marble mystery. This has been the best vacation ever!"

•—•—•

Elizabeth sat at the kitchen table, chin propped on her elbow, flipping through a library book. She loved to read, but reading was all she had done during the past week. One more week, and her grounding would be over.

"Hello, princess. What are you reading?" her father asked as he came into the kitchen.

"It's a book about an Amish girl named Rachel Yoder. I'm a little over halfway through," she told him.

He pulled out a chair and sat down across from her. "Did I ever tell you how proud I am of you?" he asked.

Elizabeth smiled but said nothing. He had told her many times.

"You are like those marbles you found—rare and precious. I'm proud of you for being so determined to help Megan and her mom," he told her.

"It was kind of fun, looking back on it. Maybe I'll be a detective someday," she said with a laugh.

He leaned forward and rested his arms on the table. "Ruby told me that you offered to use your prize money to buy Megan's band instrument. That was very generous of you."

Elizabeth blushed. She hadn't meant for others to find out. "I didn't need the money, and they did. It was no big deal."

"God loves a cheerful giver, you know," he told her, reaching out to pat her hand.

"I know—2 Corinthians 9:7," she said.

Mr. Anderson smiled at his daughter before standing up and mussing her hair. "Like I said, princess, I'm proud of you. By the way, your computer screen shows that you have e-mail waiting."

Elizabeth wasted no time in moving to the computer and clicking on her e-mail. It was from Alexis, addressed to all the Camp Club Girls.

I'm going to the London Bridge! Did you all know they moved it, and it's not in London anymore? It is at Lake Havasu, Arizona. Isn't that the craziest thing you've ever heard?

My grandmother is going to be a guest speaker at the London Bridge Festival there, at the end of October. And she's invited me to go along! I'm so excited!

Elizabeth read back through the e-mail a couple of times. *Lake Havasu. Lake Havasu.* Why did that name sound familiar?

Suddenly, she remembered. "Uh, Dad?" she called over her shoulder. "You know that convention or whatever that you go to at the end of October every year? Isn't that at Lake Havasu, Arizona?"

"Yes, it is. It's during the London Bridge Festival there. Why do you ask?"

Elizabeth felt the excitement mounting inside her. She was almost afraid to ask her next question. "Any chance I could go with you this year?"

"Funny you should ask that. I've been thinking about taking the whole family. I think you'd enjoy it."

Elizabeth lunged from her chair and threw her arms around her father's neck. "Oh, thank you, Daddy! Thank you, thank you, thank you!"

Surprised, he laughed and returned the hug. "Whoa! You're welcome! You want to tell me what this is about?"

"I will in a minute. First, I have to e-mail Alexis!"

If you enjoyed

ELIZABETH'S AMARILLO ADVENTURE

be sure to read other

CAMP CLUB GIRLS

books from BARBOUR PUBLISHING

Book 1: Mystery at Discovery Lake

Book 2: Sydney's DC Discovery

Book 3: McKenzie's Montana Mystery

Book 4: Alexis and the Sacramento Surprise

Book 5: Kate's Philadelphia Frenzy

Book 6: Bailey's Peoria Problem

AVAILABLE WHEREVER BOOKS ARE SOLD.